GRAVNICK

By Bob Herpe

Best Wishes,

Bob Herpe

NOTE

This is a work of fiction. Names, characters, places and incidents are a product of the author's imagination. Locales and public names are sometimes used for atmospheric purposes. Any resemblance to actual people, living or dead, or businesses, companies, events, institutions, or locales is completely coincidental.

ISBN 978-1-5154-1723-1
Copyright 2019 by Bob Herpe

Cover and interior design by NRK Designs

Cover photography by Rye Jessen

For information, contact www.iriebooks.com

IRIE
BOOKS

IN MEMORY OF RUSTY

CONTENTS

CHAPTER ONE

Ernie Gravnick opened the front door to his apartment and his cell phone started a round of dog barks. He had changed sirens for barks. Dogs and cops were on the same team. But somehow, he knew. He always knew. This incoming was an annoyance he didn't need. He barked back at the phone and tossed it on the couch.

He had spent most of his afternoon at the Deerfield Nursing Home, as he had every Sunday for the past seven years. Every Sunday, that is, when he wasn't called to his office at the Police Department.

It was seven years ago to the day, that Dora Gravnick suffered a stroke that left her almost totally paralyzed from the neck down. And yet her mind remained as sharp as a tack, and her tongue equally as barbed.

"I don't know why you waste your time coming around here? I don't need you. Besides, this place smells of shitty diapers. You'd do better to find yourself a nice girl to spend time with — someone pretty, that smells good. Take her nice places. Not like this piss pot."

Ernie ignored his mother's excitable moments and doted upon her. He felt personally responsible for her situation, though he would, no doubt, have been just as devoted, if circumstances had been different.

The insistent cellphone dog barks brought Ernie back from his momentary reverie. "Yeah, Gravnick here. This had better be good."

"Sorry, boss," the apologetic voice said. "We've got a real disaster on our hands." It was Jack Dilly, Gravnick's second in command at the Highland Park Homicide Department. Gravnick, also served as acting Chief of Police, with the Chief on medical leave.

"Jesus, Dilly, can't you handle it? I just walked in. I'm totally beat and I want to see the Bulls game right now."

"This one really needs you, boss. We're out at the Winton-Wilder place following up on a 911 call. You know, the Winton Cosmetics/Wilder Advertising muckety-mucks?"

Gravnick was well aware of who they were. Hell, the whole world knew.

"Yeah right, so what ya got?"

"It's bad. Two bodies, one male, mid-forties; one female, a little younger, blood all over the place. The man's hacked up. Head all but severed. Woman's been beaten to a pulp."

"Wilders?"

"Seems that way, faces are badly messed up, but pretty sure it's them."

"What about the Wilder kid?"

"Found him in the bedroom with the bodies. Just sitting there, rocking back and forth. Hasn't spoken a word — though the dispatcher said he was the one called 911."

"Boss, when this gets out, the press is going to be all over it."

"Yeah, crap. Why can't we ever get a perp who's into basketball? One with a little consideration, when there's a good game on?" Gravnick said, letting out a deep breath.

"Well?"

"Alright, I'll be there," Ernie said. "Fifteen minutes or so. Don't let anyone touch anything."

"You got it, Boss"

Ernie punched off his cell phone and headed for the bottle of Scotch he kept on the breakfast bar. After pouring himself a double shot, he sipped the soothing warmth. This was the ritual he always followed after visiting the nursing home. He needed it to wash away the stink of stale urine and old people. He swallowed the scotch and hit redial on his phone. When Dilly answered, Gravnick said, "Send a car to pick me up. I'm having a couple of drinks."

—◦⊙◦—

When Dora married Jesse Gravnick, her father, reputed Mafia Don, Caesar Casilone, immediately disowned her. Jesse was a practicing Jew and Casilone was unable to accept that *the treasure of my life* had married outside the Catholic faith. Dora was heartbroken. She idolized her father and never believed all those lies the news media concocted about him. He was the gentlest and most caring man she had ever known. But, at thirty, long after most of her contemporaries were married with kids in school, Dora had known few suitors who hadn't been scared off by her father's reputation, or directly by him, because they were "no good for you."

She had met Jesse in the super market. At just under five foot, she had been standing on her tiptoes trying to reach a box of matzo ball mix on the top shelf when everything tumbled down atop of her. Her father loved matzo ball soup and often told her there must have been some Jewish blood in his family somewhere down the line. Dora dutifully made matzo ball soup for him at least once a month.

As he came around the corner of the aisle, Jesse spotted the damsel in distress and quickly rescued her from the sea of boxes. To Dora, he seemed like Moses parting the Red Sea, as he gathered her up and out of the path of the roiling fury. Checking that she was not seriously hurt, he introduced himself. He saw that she was holding the matzo ball mix and he inquired if she was Jewish.

"No," she said. "It's for my father."

"Oh." Jesse said. "Then your father is Jewish?"

"No, we are both Catholic. My father just happens to like matzo ball soup. He has a friend that always invites him for the Jewish holidays and he has become addicted."

They laughed and continued to chat right through the check-out line into the parking lot. Then they were standing by her car. That was the beginning of their courtship.

At the time, Caesar Casilone showed an immediate liking for the young man who had so dramatically rescued his Dora. He learned that Jesse was an exceptional chess player, a game he idolized. The Don would invite him to their house on weekends and the two of them could sit by the hour, totally immersed in the game. So much so, that Dora often complained.

Over a period of the next several months Jesse became a fixture in the Casilone home. When he wasn't spending time with Dora, strolling in the Roman gardens which encompassed several acres inside the walled Casilone compound, he could be found in the Don's study or out on the poolside patio where the two men measured their game skills.

It naturally fell to Jesse to become Dora's constant companion wherever they went, and with never a hint of objection from her father. That was until Jesse asked the Don for his daughter's hand in marriage.

The outrage that beset Caesar Casilone, was akin to Mt. Etna erupting. To him Jesse Gravnick had been a toy to be played with, a pet for Dora. The idea that he could ever have serious feelings for her was more than Caesar Casilone could accept. That his daughter was in love with Jesse was totally inconceivable to him.

Not that he had anything against Jews. One of his best friends was Jewish and through the years, some of his most loyal soldiers had been Jews. But he could never allow Dora to marry someone who wasn't Catholic. Jesse was told never to visit or speak to Dora again. No threat of bodily harm was made, but there was no doubt in Jesse's mind as to the intent of Don Casilone's words.

Dora was surprised when Jesse stopped coming by the house. He didn't answer his phone when she tried calling him. Since their first meeting, they spoke to each other several times a day, especially during the week when he was busy at work in his Uncle Sol's furniture store. But when she mentioned it to her father, he just said, "Forget about him." Questioned further, he said "Yeah, came around the other day while you were out — wanted my permission to ask you to marry him."

"What did you say?" she asked.

"I told him no, of course. I knew you'd never consider marrying anyone who wasn't Catholic."

"Daddy, how could you?"

She turned on him like a wild animal. She used words she would never say to anyone. She even jabbed with her sharp fingernails. When she had finished, she turned and walked out of the house. That night Dora and Jesse caught a plane to Las Vegas and were married in The Garden of Love Wedding Chapel.

When the Don heard about this, his first thought was to put out a hit on Jesse. His second thought was to disown Dora and leave them be. Actually, his love for his daughter kept him from doing anything to further estrange her from him.

Over the next two years, Dora heard nothing of or about her father, except from the slander printed in the newspapers, or the talking heads on television. That was just fine with her. For Jesse the silence was a questionable reprieve that left him constantly wondering. Meanwhile, completely unknown to them, everything that happened in their lives was immediately reported back to Caesar Casilone through a carefully concealed network of watchful eyes and ears.

CHAPTER TWO

E rnie Gravnick came to this upscale Chicago suburb of Highland Park following a successful career as a detective in the Windy City's homicide division
where he earned a reputation as a smart, hard-nosed cop. Trained as an attorney,
he'd also been a prosecutor for Cook County. This didn't last long. Political gamesmanship was not his game.

Gravnick arrived at the palatial Wilder home at exactly 9:00 p.m. The front
door was open and guarded by an officer who pointed him at the stairway to the
master bedroom. Upstairs Ernie saw Dilly, who took him aside and began detail-
ing the murder scene.

"We got here at 8:07 to find the front door wide open. Blood smears on
the door and all the way up the stair casing, as you no doubt noticed."

"Yup."

"When we entered the bedroom, we spotted the kid sitting over there,
rocking just as he is now."

"We absolutely sure it's the Wilders?"

"We'll get positive IDs, but there's not much doubt."

"Medical examiner here yet?"

"Yeah, Mac just arrived. He's looking at the bodies now."

"You'll note the hatchet…blood on it…"

Ernie glanced at the blood-covered blade, as well as the blunt hammer end
of the hatchet. The handle was also blood-spattered, except for the area where it

had been gripped.

"We got pictures of everything," Dilly said. "Nothing is touched. That's it,"

Mac McCarthy's voice broke in. "I think I have something."

The room fell silent as the medical examiner reaffixed his stethoscope to the woman victim's carotid artery.

"Yeah, barely discernable, but the female's got a slight pulse. Let's move on it, people."

The EMT's moved quickly. After carefully slipping a brace beneath the victim's neck and upper back, they placed a mask on the woman's face, and began pumping oxygen into the victim's lungs. Then, attaching IV lines, the body was put on a body board.

Gravnick moved to the boy sitting nearby.

Jonathan Birch Wilder, dutiful 13-year-old son of Thornton B. Wilder and Julie Winton-Wilder, sat trance-like, on the edge of an oversized, tufted ottoman, rocking back and forth. As Gravnick gently approached him, a low humming sound came from the boy's lips.

"This is for Children's Protective Services," Gravnick told Dilly. For a while he studied him. The boy was tall for his age. He appeared awkward when the officer led him from the room. Gravnick remembered seeing something about the kid's cleverness with a camera. Even at this young age, he'd established himself as a budding landscape photographer. He had even won some regional awards.

It was the next day before the family attorney officially identified Thornton Wilder's body. Testing of the weapon showed no fingerprints on the hatchet but, the handle revealed traces of latex, leading police to believe that the perpetrator wore gloves. However, no gloves were immediately found. A check of the open front door also proved negative for prints — even those of the family, which normally would have been found there. Someone had obviously wiped them clean.

Transferred to a psychiatric trauma center by Child Protective Services, the boy remained silent and stone-faced for the next five days, before gradually regaining his ability to speak. However, he appeared unable to remember anything about the incident that took place in his parent's bedroom. The police psychologist informed Gravnick that there was no telling how long it might take for the boy to regain his memory — if indeed he ever would.

Meanwhile, his mother, barely alive and completely comatose, remained in intensive care in Highland Park Community Hospital.

CHAPTER THREE

When Dora Gravnick gave birth to healthy baby boy, Don Casilone was in tears. It was the boy he had long dreamed of. He laughed one moment, cried the next. Those who were with him at the time, his trusted aides, had never witnessed the Don, in such a state of crazy joy. They realized it was the flip side of his insane remorse when his daughter had walked out on him.

But he would change that. He showed up, hat in hand, at the open door of Dora's hospital room. There before him sat Dora, baby to her breast. Standing next to her was Jesse. It was the perfect family picture. For the second time that day, Don Casilone cried as he begged their forgiveness.

With the arrival of baby Ernie into the family, life resumed as if nothing untoward ever happened between the members of the Casilone family. At her father's pleading, Dora and Jesse moved out of their small west side flat into one of the five houses on the Casilone compound. Evenings were spent with Caesar and Jesse at the chess table, and Dora reading anything she could dig up on child care. She also made matzo ball soup on the first Friday of every month.

As Ernie grew into an active toddler, Don Casilone insisted on babysitting. This was his opportunity to bond with his grandson. Ernie loved these special times with his Poppee. It was the beginning of a true friendship. Every spare moment found them doing something fun together. By the time Ernie was six, the Don was amazed by his grandson's quick mind and physical coordination. As for Ernie, he couldn't get enough of the Don's outrageous stories.

Ernie was now becoming quite a chess player, occasionally beating Poppee at his own game. When he was eight, he was already a crack shot with a 22 caliber target rifle, at Poppee's shooting range. At nine, his score rose to ten out of ten, even when firing one-handed, while riding by the target at full gallop on one of Poppee's fine horses.

That's the way it was right up until that fateful day. It was a Saturday, a day off from school where Ernie was a bright, eager fifth grader. He had been after Poppee to take him to the Brookfield Zoo. His teacher had told his class about how the animals there were not kept in cages: they roamed around outside in natural habitats. This was the day they had planned to go.

So while Dora stayed home, Caesar Casilone, Jesse and Ernie made the excursion to Chicago's south side. They were accompanied by two of the Don's most trusted body guards. When Ernie asked why, Poppee said, "Because bad people are jealous of my success in business." He left it at that.

At the zoo, the shaded greenery of the African rain forest gave Ernie a real thrill. The eeriness of it was both scary and exciting. Ernie's imagination ran wild. He spotted the velvety brown coat of an Okapi caught in a patch of sunlight and a bright flash of scarlet red that was the plumage of the Lady Ross Turaco as it took off in flight. His teacher said the creature was so-named by the famed arctic explorer Admiral Cook, after his wife, Lady Ross Cook.

A short time later, as Ernie emerged into a sunlit area of the park, his attention was drawn to an exhibit on the left. Behind him, shielding their eyes from the sudden burst of sunlight, Caesar, Jesse and the rest of their entourage failed to see the boy dart into the gathering crowd. The onlookers were watching the antics of the red haired orangutans.

Suddenly there came the rattle of automatic weapons. When the gunfire finished, two bodyguards lay dead, and Jesse, limp and bloodied, had fallen on top of the lifeless body of Don Caesar Casilone.

The gun smoke was still suspended in the air when Ernie ran to his father. Then he saw his grandfather underneath him. Ernie cried out. "I'm sorry, Poppee. I'm sorry."

It was not until after the police paramedics arrived and took him away that Ernie stopped crying. Even then, heartbroken and shaking, he believed he alone was responsible for the death of his father and grandfather. *They came to this place because of me.*

Upon examination of the bodies, the paramedics found a faint remnant of life flickered in Jesse. Ten days later, he died in a hospital, but not before waking long enough to say goodbye to his beloved Dora and making Ernie promise to care for his mother for as long as she lived.

Dora tried her best to become a steadying hand for Ernie. That was until sometime later when the IRS seized all of her assets inherited from the Don, including the properties that made up the whole of the Casilone compound. With that, mother and son found themselves out on the street. They had only the clothes on their backs. But also an unbreakable trust fund — Don Caesar Casilone's parting gift, ensuring his grandson's education.

CHAPTER FOUR

With the press clamoring for action and pressure coming from the mayor, the governor and even the White House, due to the Winton family's political ties, Gravnick found himself being peppered from all sides. He was used to such pressure-cooker situations, often associated with his job in Chicago. That is the main reason he didn't think twice about taking his present position, as Chief of Detectives in this North Shore suburb.

Sure, there was an occasional murder or unexplained death, even here, but nothing ever on the scale of the Winton-Wilder case. These were two of the area's most celebrated residents and no one was about to let this one rest. Yet, he had to admit he was totally stumped. All he could do was have his people go back over the crime scene until something showed up. There was no such thing as a perfect crime in Gravnick's book. "Bad guys always screwed up somewhere."

The following two and a half weeks, were like an eternity to Gravnick. The press hounded him, his crime cops combed every inch of the Wilder home many times, and still, nothing was found that implicated anyone.

Meanwhile, Gravnick interviewed business associates, friends and known enemies of the victims. By the middle of the third week of the investigation, the Highland Park Crime scene had yielded nothing. A further search of the Wilder house came up dry. They'd gone over every inch of the place and found nothing.

"Go over it a hundred times," Gravnick said. "Then maybe I'll believe there's nothing to be found." On Thursday of that week, after some really hot chili, a crime scene tech needed to use the toilet. Although this was against police policy, the tech couldn't help it — he ran to the off-limits bathroom.

After fifteen minutes of grunts and groans, the man emerged with a more than curious grin on. In his hand was a wad of toilet tissue, which he held up for all to see, loudly exclaiming "Got something."

Unfolding the tissue, he revealed surgical gloves, immersed in what looked like, the contents found in a baby's diarrhea-filled diaper. "When I flushed the toilet," he explained, "water began backing up and overflowed the bowl. There was a toilet plunger under the sink cabinet, and I used it. That's when the suspect gloves got dislodged."

The lab reclaimed barely perceptible smudges of what appeared to be the user's fingerprints. The gloves revealed three separate traces of DNA. Naturally one of the samples bore traces of chili peppers. That aside, the discovery of the gloves was the first real break in the case.

CHAPTER FIVE

Little by little, Jonathan Wilder regained bits and pieces of his memory. However, a full month had gone by before he was able to recall any of the terrible incidents that had taken place in his parent's bedroom.

Under questioning by Gravnick in the presence of a police psychologist and the boy's grandmother, who the court had assigned as temporary guardian, the boy described:

"On that day, it was a Sunday, my parents and I hung around together all day. I remember because, it was the first time we had spent time with each other in weeks. Mom and Dad were always busy with work, or some kind of outside meetings.

"They had given the household help the day off and the three of us went in to downtown Chicago, to see an exhibit of photographic art, at the Art Institute. It was a really super showing of Ansel Adams' work. He's one of my favorites. Then, we had an early dinner out before returning home."

"What time was that?" Gravnick asked.

"About 7:15 p.m. After that I was working in my dark room in the basement until exactly nine o'clock."

"How are you so sure about the time?"

"That's the curfew my father set for me on school nights. He was very strict about it."

Jonathan went on to say, he heard nothing while in the darkroom, that it's totally sound proof. Gravnick made a note to check it out.

"I emerged from the basement stairwell," Jonathan said, "and went through the kitchen into the front hallway on my way upstairs to get ready for bed."

"What did you do then?" Gravnick asked

"When I entered the hall to the foyer, I noticed that the front door was wide open. "I figured that one of my parents was probably out front, went to the door and called out to them. Nobody answered, so I stepped out and looked around."

"How long were you out there?"

"Maybe three, four minutes, I guess. Then I came back in and ran upstairs, continuing to call to my parents."

"Was there a reason you didn't close the front door when you came in?"

The boy stood dumbfounded. He really couldn't explain why he left the door open.

"Okay." Gravnick said. "So, you ran upstairs. What did you do then?"

"When there was no answer, I went to my parent's bedroom at the other end of the hallway. Seeing that the door was wide open, I began to think something might be wrong."

"Why was that?"

"They were very private people. They never left their door open."

"Go on."

"When I got to the doorway and saw a chair upturned and their personal things scattered all over, I got real scared."

Gravnick noticed some shakiness in the boy's voice and offered him a few moments to recover. He seemed truly upset as he relived the memory. After the short pause, Jonathan continued. "Then I saw them. They were just lying there on the floor, all covered with blood." He began crying, this time hysterically.

After giving the boy time to calm down, Ernie queried. "Are you okay Jonathan?"

He nodded. "Yes."

"Okay, what did you do then?"

"Everything's a blur. I'm really not sure what happened then. At first, I couldn't think of what to do. It was maybe ten minutes before I thought about calling 911."

Gravnick asked Jonathan if he had ever seen any surgical or examination gloves in the house. Did he know of anyone who might have wanted to harm his mother or father?

He responded no to both questions.

After excusing Jonathan and the others, Gravnick sat, deep in thought. Something about the boy's story bothered him. Ernie picked up the empty coke bottle the boy had been drinking from and put it into a Ziplock. Back at the lab he would ask them to compare the boy's DNA with that on the gloves.

Gravnick kept digging, but there was still very little to go on. He did pick up something from a business associate of Julie Wilder's. She told him that Mrs. Wilder had shown some concern after discovering several larger than usual blocks of Winton stock had been bought up.

But they appeared to be totally unrelated to each other, and there was no proof that it meant anything.

A few days later the crime scene lab handed Gravnick the first piece of what seemed like solid evidence. One of the DNA samples found on the examination gloves did indeed belong to Jonathan — the other strangely matched up to Julie Wilder. Unfortunately, the boy's response was not helpful. He suddenly recalled his mother sometimes used latex gloves when applying her makeup, and that at one time he himself had tried them on.

"This happened some time ago and how they could have ended up in the downstairs toilet, I don't know," he said.

Gravnick's head was spinning. Was it just nervousness under questioning? Yet, there were other things …

The boy had sufficient opportunity, and appeared physically capable, of implementing these crimes. He was definitely a little different and obviously spoiled by parents, too busy to give him the personal time he apparently craved. Also, according to his teachers and the household servants, the kid was somewhat of a loner.

Still, Gravnick remained on edge about a possible motive. Though Jonathan had some eccentricities, the boy exhibited absolutely no dislike for either parent. In fact he expressed elation over spending the day with them at the Art Institute and dining together. For, him to have committed such a heinous act, would have required a buildup of sheer hate over a long period of time. It didn't add up.

The State Attorney ignored Gravnick's warning, that the evidence was mostly circumstantial. He made the decision to go forward, if for no other reason than to get the press off of their backs. A few days later the grand jury moved to indict Jonathan Wilder, charging him with the murder of his father and the attempted murder of his mother. But, Gravnick had not missed the State Attorney's warning —"Find me something to nail this case down with."

Chapter Six

As Dora's pride did not allow her to ask for help, the first weeks of their exile were spent in a shelter on Chicago's West Madison Street — Skid Row. At first, she left the shelter early each morning in an effort to find work. It was still summer and school would not start up for another few weeks. Gravnick volunteered at the shelter helping others clean up the daily residuum of society's outcasts. The odor of fatty foods and decaying souls hung in the foetid air of the desolate place. He also helped out in the soup kitchen and did whatever else he could. It was a learning experience he would long remember. He didn't get paid of course, but it kept him busy while his mother was away.

Unfortunately, without work experience, or any specialized skills, and no permanent address, Dora was unable to find a steady job. With only odd job money coming in, Dora soon became morose and withdrawn. Gravnick tried to keep her spirits up, but to no avail. She began going out later, and returning earlier.

As summer was ending and school began, he pleaded with his mother: "Call someone. A relative. A friend. Let someone help. Please Mama." Still Dora refused to give in.

Not willing to accept their plight, Gravnick talked himself into an off-the-books job, sweeping up and running errands at a neighborhood pool hall. He did this each day after school, which his mother insisted he attend. The money he earned was immediately turned over to her.

The pool hall was owned by an old friend and associate of Poppee's, Willie, The Moose, Gavanno, so named, because his face was long like that of a moose. The story is that his mother had a hard time giving birth to Willie. Also her second-rate doctor applied too much pressure extracting him from her womb, literally molding his face into a bulbous snout.

Though Gravnick was legally too young to work, Gavanno never worried about such things. The beat cops were on his payroll and no one dared report him.

He became a fixture around the pool hall. Everyone loved him. He was smart and never got in anyone's way. Most of all, Gravnick was a good listener, a trait that would serve him well in his future professions as a prosecutor and later as a cop.

Little by little, he began picking up hints of what really went down that day at Brookfield Zoo. The day his father and grandfather were gunned down in front of him. The day, he could never, and would never, forget.

The name Sal Giaconte began popping up in conversations among the patrons. This was a name Gravnick had heard on occasion, while visiting at Poppee's house. From his grandfather's actions at the time, he suspected Giaconte had not been one of his grandfather's favorite people.

Gravnick continued working and listening. Over the next several weeks, the pieces seemed to fall in place. The unofficial word on the street was that Salvatore Giaconte had put out the hit on Don Casilone.

Giaconte had a small piece of the Southside action, garnered over a period of time, for his loyalty to Don Franko Pistale, the man who ran the Southside for years. For Giaconte, it wasn't enough. He was ambitious. He wanted more. He wanted it all. His intent was to get Caesar Cassilone out of the way, then move in and take over the Westside. Once established as the "Man-in-Charge," he would take the remainder of the Southside from the aging Don Pistale.

As young and inexperienced as Gravnick was, his instincts told him, these stories were not enough. Proof was going to be needed, before the authorities would listen, or do anything. Because of his age, no one would listen anyway.

Having learned this much, young Ernie Gravnick vowed to do whatever it took to avenge the deaths of his father and grandfather — A decision that was to define the future course of his life.

Returning to the shelter one evening, he found that Dora could hardly stand up. She had obviously been drinking. Something she had been doing more of lately. The next day, unbeknownst to his mother, Gravnick contacted his father's Uncle Sol, who immediately insisted they move to his plush Libertyville horse farm, with his wife Sylvia and him. Dora was livid with Ernie for disobeying her orders. But after much pleading and guilt-laying from Uncle Sol about subjecting Ernie to the outrages of living on the street, Dora reluctantly agreed. Always the politician, Sol assured her that she could make it up to them, once she got on her feet. To help get her started, he offered her a job at his furniture store.

CHAPTER SEVEN

Gravnick's educational years followed in rapid though distinguished succession. Living outside of the school district, with special dispensation obtained through Uncle Sol's political connections, he was allowed to attend highly rated New Trier Township High. He completed high school in just three years after acing the college qualifiers. At the same time, proving his athletic prowess, Gravnick broke the all-time record for pass completions, as the New Trier Trevian's ace quarterback.

Totally focused on what he had vowed to do, Gravnick proceeded to turn down several scholarship opportunities to play college football. Instead, using Poppee's inheritance, he devoted himself to the study of pre-law at the University of Northwestern, to which he was readily accepted. Upon graduating cum laude from Northwestern and earning a law degree at the University of Chicago, where he excelled as editor of the Law Review, and was entered into the "Order of The Coif," Gravnick accepted a position as a prosecutor in the State Attorney's office in Cook County.

⁓⊙⊙⁓

By the time Ernie had come to the Cook County State Attorney's office, Sal Giaconte was well in control of Chicago's Westside. As a prosecutor, Gravnick went after the new Don with a vengeance. But each time something meaningful appeared in the offing, Ernie seemed to be thwarted by the SA, whom he came to suspect was being paid off by Giaconte. Though unable to prove any such relationship existed between the two, he soon tired of the political gamesmanship surrounding the prosecutor's office. It was barely two years later that Ernie resigned to join the Chicago Police Department.

Meanwhile over the years, Dora had never been able to shake off the terrible deaths of her beloved Jesse and her father. Though Uncle Sol and Aunt Sylvia had been wonderful to both she and Ernie, and had gone out of their way to help Dora handle her bouts of depression, something she expressed gratefulness for, she remained haunted by memories, and continued to drown her sorrows in alcohol. It was during one of her weekend binges that she suffered the debilitating stroke that had left her a complete invalid.

The effect of this event only reinforced Gravnick's feelings of him being directly responsible. *Had I not made Poppee take me to the Brookfield Zoo, he and my father would still be alive and my mother would not have suffered the sadness that led to her stroke.* Because of this, as well as his promise to his father to always look after her, Gravnick made it his mission to spend as much time as he could with his mother.

Gravnick's career with the Department proved to be rewarding. Insisting that he be shown no preference because of his legal background and experience as a prosecutor, Gravnick hit the streets as a beat cop learning the ropes the hard way. Only after serving in uniform for a period of time did he attempt the Detectives Exam. This he aced first time around after which he was assigned to a special investigations unit.

After a new, progressive, State Attorney was seated, Ernie eventually got an indictment and a guilty verdict against Giaconte — not for the murders of his father and grandfather, but on multiple drug and money laundering charges.

During the course of his investigation, Gravnick sensed that someone higher up might actually have given the order for the hit on his grandfather. That perhaps Giaconte wasn't the only one responsible. He might well have been used as a front, to hide the real source. Could the West Side have been his reward? Not just to shut him up, but providing you curb any ideas you might have, of grabbing more territory?

Still, try as he might, Ernie was unable to turn his suspicion into anything more. He began to believe that his hunch was just that, a hunch and nothing more. It was not until many years later that Ernie's suspicions were to return, then totally by accident while investigating a completely unrelated case.

CHAPTER EIGHT

After several months, Julie Wilder awakened from her coma. With daily therapy and dogged determination, she slowly recovered from her ordeal. Learning that her son was being held on murder charges and confronted with the State's apparent evidence against him, she revealed a scenario that threw doubt on their entire case.

"We returned home that evening after spending a pleasant day with our son Jonathan. Suddenly my husband confronted me, saying it was he who was behind the buying up of my company's stock. His scheme was to separately gather up enough of the company's stock, so when combined, they would represent a controlling interest in Winton Cosmetics, Inc.

Then with a look of unbridled anger that I never knew him capable of, he sneered and said, 'And now my darling wife, with that accomplished, I am ready to execute a takeover of your beloved company. Oh, and though I really don't require them, I've decided to do you a huge favor. Before we make the official announcement, I'm going give you an opportunity to sell all of your shares to me. This will allow you to save that pretty face of yours from any embarrassment.' His reason was that he could no longer stand being 'Julie Winton's number two.'

"It seemed that no matter how great his own successes had been, he was convinced others saw him merely as Julie's lap dog. Then he showed me what a sick bastard he really was."

"To me, our marriage has never been anything but a business arrangement.

However, as long as you cooperate, by selling out, I'll be happy to continue the charade of being the loving husband and family man. You can merely issue a statement that you are tired of the pressures of business and wish to stay at home for a while and raise our sensitive and extremely talented son. No one on the outside will ever question you."

Julie, now showing emotion for the first time since beginning her story —"How could I have lived and worked with that man all these years, and never suspect who he really was? He fooled me completely."

"And then what happened?" Gravnick asked.

Julie told him, "Upon hearing this, I just stomped out of the room and walked directly downstairs to the basement storage area, where I knew Thornton kept his hunting gear, including a hatchet.

"Returning to the bedroom," Julie said, "I found him sitting on the ottoman reading through some papers, like nothing had happened. As he looked up, totally unconcerned, I walked straight to him holding the hatchet hidden behind my back and gave him my answer; 'Fuck you, you bastard.'

"Then, as I brought my arm up, with the intent of — chopping the son-of-a-bitch's head off — someone, or something, grabbed me from behind. With my arm held in what felt like a steel vice, I heard a cracking sound. My right arm was broken. In spite of the pain, I somehow continued to strike out in every way possible, using my other arm, my feet, my head, even my shoulders in an attempt to get loose from what was holding me. But my efforts proved futile, as more and more blows assailed me. After that I just passed out. But don't doubt it for a minute, whoever killed my husband did me a favor. If I hadn't been stopped, I had every intention of killing him myself."

A few weeks later, testifying in court on behalf of Jonathan, Julie stated:

"Though I have no idea of who killed my husband, I do know it could not have been my son. It is true Jonathan is a big boy for his age, but he's also the least athletic kid you'll ever know. While other children his age are out playing, Jonathan has always been one to spend his time shooting pictures or working in his dark room. Involving himself in intellectual pursuits is as stimulating an activity as he ever allows himself. Getting him to actually move his body, or do anything physical in nature, let alone partake in exercise or physical sports, has been the bane of our relationship with our son. In other words, Johnathan represents the ultimate blob.

"On the other hand, as the press has often made much-too-much of, having gone so far as to compare my physical strength to that of the average man, I have always sought to maintain a high peak of physical and athletic ability. Yet, whoever grabbed my arm and disabled me that evening, displayed strength and athleticism far beyond the average. Beyond anything my son is possibly capable of."

Next morning after bringing the court to order, Judge Julian West announced that the State's case against Jonathan Birch Wilder was being dropped for lack of evidence.

Reviewing what happened so far, Gravnick turned his attention to Thornton Wilder and his associates. Who was Wilder, really? He needed to know more. If Julie's story about her husband trying to take over her company was true, and it certainly seemed to be a logical explanation for what had happened, where did he get the money from? As successful as his own business was, it was still small time compared to Winton Cosmetics. Wilder did not have the kind of funds required to buy such a large quantity of the publicly traded company's stock.

Who were his investors? Would any of them have had a motive for killing Wilder? Maybe Wilder decided to hold up the investors for a bigger piece of the action? If Wilder was becoming a liability they may have decided to take him out and take over Winton Cosmetics for themselves: What if they decided to kill both Wilder and his wife and, in the attempt, only thought they had killed Julie? After all, the police themselves were unable to detect any signs of life when first arriving on the scene.

That would answer the question of what really happened to her. On the other hand, Julie Winton's out-front personality was so identified with the company that removing her could greatly impede the company's business. Getting rid of her didn't make any sense. There were still too many unknowns.

In order to learn more about Wilder, Gravnick repeatedly questioned Julie Winton-Wilder. How did you meet him? Where did he come from? Who were his associates? The more time he spent picking her brain, the more Ernie became convinced that her story could not have been made up. The facts of her confession were indeed persuasive. Then again, Julie Winton was an unusual woman with a sharp mind. As the CEO of a multinational beauty and cosmetic conglomerate and a recognized celebrity, she was used to thinking on her feet. Once faced with the evidence against her son, it would be no big deal for her to concoct such a story.

CHAPTER NINE

Born Sean Patrick Connelly, Thornton Wilder grew up in Brooklyn, NY. The product of a father, a sometimes construction worker when not too drunk to stand up, and a mother who cleaned houses of the well-to-do. That is, when the swelling on her face healed enough from the beatings endured from her abusive husband. His sister Katherene, twelve years his elder, left home by the time he was four years old, having been disowned by her father after, as he put it, "getting herself knocked up by a black-assed nigger from Bedford Stuyvesant."

On his thirteenth birthday, though threatened many times, Sean received the first beating from his father. It was his last. The next day, he ran away from home and went to live with his sister. He had secretly stayed in contact with her through the years. Sean knew that after miscarrying in her seventh month, she had moved to Newark, New Jersey, to live with a sometimes boyfriend. He never saw either of his parents again.

In high school, Sean displayed a talent for writing and art. By his senior year, these talents, along with a boyish smile and an almost manic desire to succeed, led him to an internship at a local advertising agency. Upon graduation, he was hired there as a copywriter.

While working for the agency he wrote a book, *The Entrepreneur's Guide to Marketing and Advertising*. For this purpose he used the pseudonym, Thornton Wilder. Stealing the name of the great Pulitzer winning author made him feel like someone special. But when his editor argued against the use of the name, his compromise was to add the middle name Burnett: Thornton Burnett Wilder, a name he would soon adopt officially, upon moving out from his sister and her druggie friend. A move designed to erase any semblance of his roots.

In short order, Wilder's book became must-reading in business circles, and was soon adopted as a text by many top business schools. Within a year and a half after graduating high school, every well-known ad agency in New York was courting him.

Carefully plotting his future, he accepted a position as an assistant account executive and chief copywriter with Prentice, Keene and Margolin, known in Madison Avenue circles as PKM. It was there, while sitting in on an agency presentation, pitching the Winton Cosmetics account, that Thornton came to the attention of the famed and wealthy Julie Winton.

Though headquartered in Chicago, Winton had made no bones about her unhappiness with the focus of her present agency's ad campaign. She was in New York shopping for the best of the best. She wanted new ideas and new blood. She was pitting the industry's key players against each other.

Verne McCauley, the president of PKM, was himself handling the Winton presentation, into which the firm had invested a great deal of time and money. But as McCauley droned on, Thornton could see Julie Winton beginning to lose patience with his boss's blowhard spiel.

Jumping up, he walked directly to the head of the long boardroom table, rudely interrupting his boss in mid-sentence. "I'm sorry sir, but I believe Miss Winton is looking for something totally different. If you don't mind, let me throw out some concepts I believe just might interest her."

McCauley turned almost purple. "How dare you interrupt me? Who in hell do you think you are?" he shouted. "Get this piece of shit out of my sight and don't ever, let me see him around here again."

Two of McCauley's underlings jumped up from the conference table but Julie Winton intervened. "Let him continue. I want to hear what he's got to say."

McCauley had no choice, but to let Wilder take over. With no visuals or audio, other than a white board, some crayons, and his own voice-over conceptions, Wilder proceeded to rough out an entire print campaign and a complete TV storyboard that was like none of them could ever have conceived. By the time he had finished, everyone in the room, including Verne McCauley, sat silent and awestruck by what they had just witnessed.

Getting up from the table, Julie Winton approached Thornton Wilder, grabbed him by the arm and led him out of the room, offering as an aside, "Since you no longer want him here, he's all mine."

Wilder accepted Julie's offer to start an in-house agency for Winton Cosmetics. He also asked for, and got, a proviso that he could take on additional, non-conflicting accounts, and that at such time that either party decided to part company, he would be able to buy out the agency, at 50% of the then appraised value. With his terms agreed to, Wilder moved to Chicago, leaving behind any appearance of where he came from.

Wilder's influence on the direction of Winton Cosmetic's marketing program was soon all encompassing. This resulted in immediate increases in sales for the company and extreme resentment from many of Winton's top brass. Wilder simply ignored and shrugged them off, as a bunch of automatons. Their antipathy meant little. Julie Winton was totally enamored by everything about the man, including his extreme good looks.

The T.B. Wilder Advertising Company took off like a rocket. One Fortune 500 company after another, witnessing the ingenious concepts proffered by Wilder, begged to be added to the firm's client list. Before long the agency occupied the entire tenth floor of the Winton Building in downtown Chicago.

Though a personal relationship with Julie Winton had become a part of his plan, Wilder played it cool. He waited for Julie to make the advances he knew she would. But Julie Winton was used to calling the shots. It took almost a year before her anticipation got the better of her.

It came about one evening after his staff people had left. Thornton was alone in his office, working on a presentation, when Julie entered unnoticed. Absorbed in what he was doing, he remained unaware of her. But then she leaned over his shoulder, and gently sticking her tongue in his ear she whispered, "I love you." In the same instant, she untied and stepped out of her wrap dress, the only thing she was wearing. Showing no surprise, Wilder slowly turned his chair and drew her naked body to him.

Thornton and Julie were married three months later. The event was attended by the finest of Chicago society, government officials, and leaders of the cosmetics industry from around the world. One year later to the day, Julie gave birth to a son — Jonathan Birch Wilder.

CHAPTER TEN

Gravnick and the Highland Park Police Department continued their investigation into the murder of Thornton Wilder. What kind of person or persons were involved? Why was he killed? Was Julie also supposed to die? Who would Wilder have turned to for money to take over his wife's company? They could not have been ordinary investors. The act required big money. Really big money. It had to be an organization with huge resources. Was it another company? Follow the money. If it had come from legitimate sources, the money must have been invested somewhere previously. Massive funds like these were never left sitting around. They needed to be kept working. Earning money all the time.

Gravnick put his resources to work. He told Jack Dilly to check on any large stock or land sales that may have taken place in recent months. Finding nothing unusual through their Wall Street contacts, the investigation spread overseas looking for any large foreign exchange deals.

Meanwhile Gravnick's doubts about Julie Winton continued to haunt him. What makes the woman tick? On the surface she seemed to have it together. She was smart, tough and had a no-nonsense approach to the world around her. But was this really who she was? He needed to dig deeper. Where did she come from? And, how did she get there?

Kneeling before King George VI, Colonel Harry Winton had a sudden sense of awe. He was an American, being knighted by the King of England, entered as an honorary member into the historic Knights of the Round Table. He already carried the gold eagles of a full Colonel in the U. S. Army on his shoulders, an accomplishment he was proud of, but the present honor somehow overcame him.

When General of the Armies, Dwight David Eisenhower, received this honor, it was easily understood. His name was widely recognized as the man who led the Allied forces that ultimately kept Europe from falling under the grasp of the Nazis. But Harry Winton? No one ever heard of him. That was until the story in the *London Times* informed the British people that if it not been for the selfless bravery of one American, the whole of the British way of life, and the success of the Allied invasion itself, could well have been lost.

Having responded to the personal and secret request of Winston Churchill, this man, who owed no allegiance to England, had undertaken a most dangerous mission. The operation took him deep inside Nazi Germany, where at great personal risk, he skillfully infiltrated the Nazi hierarchy, and carefully fed misleading information that was to find its way to the Nazi Fuehrer himself. It was this very deception that led Hitler, against the advice of his generals, to redeploy German forces away from where the Allied invasion was to actually take place. This man was Harry Winton, at the time a little known US Army colonel, assigned as a special attaché and communications link to the Prime Minister's office by General Eisenhower.

Recognition of his accomplishments won Harry immediate acclaim at home and abroad. Hearing of his feats, President Harry S. Truman issued an executive order, promoting him to the status of Brigadier General and requested he be re-assigned to special duty in Washington, DC. For the next several years Harry Winton served admirably under both President Truman and his successor Dwight D. Eisenhower, handling several highly sensitive assignments.

Following retirement from the army, Winton returned to his hometown of Chicago. There he rose to immediate prominence, easily winning a seat in the U.S. Congress. In his Illinois district, he soon built a name as a consensus maker. When his first term as a congressman was winding down, the opposition party knew that Winton was the man to beat in the next senate race. Yet, when the votes were counted, the State of Illinois had elected itself a new Senator, Sir Harry Winton. A man who would go on to distinguish himself again and again. A man who could have been President of the United States, but refused to compromise his standards to get elected.

Along the way Winton married the beautiful Jennifer Luce Vandervelt, who at the time was considered society's most eligible woman. She too had served her country, in her case as an army nurse during the war (something young ladies of her ilk didn't do back then) and had been decorated for extreme courage under fire. She also had a reputation as a mover and shaker for charitable causes around the world. The two of them were on every prominent party list in and out of Washington. In time, Jennifer gave birth to a baby boy — Harry Winton, Jr.

From the day young Harry was born, he was destined to grow up in his father's footsteps. Completing his undergraduate work in political science at the University of Chicago, and a law degree from Yale, he was easily sought after by the most prestigious law firms. Choosing the practice best suited to his needs, Harry went to work specializing in constitutional law.

As he always knew, the private side of law was not to be his destiny; it wasn't long before he threw his hat in the ring and ran for public office. Harry Winton, Jr. became one of the youngest candidates ever elected to the U.S. Congress.

The day after his election, Harry married his high school sweetheart against his parent's wishes. Her name was Jean Drexler. She was Jewish. She was a promising designer of women's clothing. But she came from a different world than Sir Harry and Jennifer Winton.

Harry Junior, knew it would be a long wait before he could seek to replace his father in the Senate. Sir Harry was a proud man. A stubborn man. He would not walk away from the limelight easily. This was particularly so, as his son and he didn't always see things eye-to-eye. However, Harry Junior was also stubborn — and he was willing to wait. At least for the time being.

In the meantime, Jean and Harry would work hard and earn their own successes. When Jean found herself with child, the couple was ecstatic over the thought of becoming parents. As her due date was approaching, Harry flew in from Washington to make sure he would be with his wife when the baby came. The morning Jean told him it was time, Harry excitedly grabbed the suitcase that had been packed and waiting. He helped his wife into the car, and off they went on their way to the hospital.

That was when a speeding truck ran a red light, smashing directly into the passenger side of the Winton's car. The EMT's found the mother, father and truck driver dead. They also noted that the impact of the crash, had miraculously forced the baby from her mother's womb. There, hanging from the umbilical cord, they found a beautiful baby girl, protesting with the strongest pair of lungs they had ever encountered. This was the setting under which Jean and Harry Winton, Jr's only child was born.

Though the baby was not something they needed or wanted, for appearances sake alone, the child was legally adopted and would be cared for by her grandparent's, Jennifer and Senator Sir Harry Winton. They called her Julie.

—◌◠—

Growing up as the advantaged child she was, Julie attended all the right schools, including Rosemary Hall and Wellesley. Having traveled these hallowed footsteps, she nevertheless remained far from the spoiled child one might expect. Actually, like both of her parents and grandparents, Julie was very much her own person, her ideas often bringing her in direct conflict with the elder Winton's.

Though her talents in the arts and English (not to mention her family name) would have offered her entrée to most any job she wanted, she craved something more — the independence that comes from being in charge of one's own destiny. This brought her to enroll in the Rollins College School of Business, where she earned an additional degree from that prestigious Winter Park, Florida institution.

After establishing the Julie Winton line of professional cosmetics, which she marketed exclusively through beauty salons in major cities throughout the country, her quest to go beyond the average brought Julie back to Rollins. With the establishment there, of the Crummer School of Business in 1980, she became among the first to complete their MBA program.

Over the next few years Julie proved herself a shrewd and resourceful business operator, deftly building a small, but successful, boutique-oriented business into an internationally known beauty and cosmetic behemoth. Perhaps the part of Julie's life that created the greatest intrigue and almost overnight turned into a living legend, was brought about by the celebrity garnered through her weekly appearances as the star of the popular TV reality show *The Beautiful You*, which she personally created and produced. The program had not only afforded an opportunity to showcase the quality and best use of Winton Cosmetics products, but through a variety of guest specialists, contestants were given coaching in makeup, hair styling, proper dress, speech and communication skills, and more.

A competition was held each week between contestants. The audience and professional Judges voted for the contestant they believe showed the greatest improvement. Weekly winners moved on to appear in the next level of competition, with a chance to go all the way for the Grand Prize. They also received valuable gifts that ranged from a year's supply of Winton Cosmetic products, to complete wardrobes.

The grand prize winner would earn the title "Winton Woman of the Year," appear as spokesperson for Winton Cosmetics in a series of Winton TV commercials, and non-stop, personal appearances in cities around the world. To go along with this stepped up status, the winner also received a luxury sports car, business expense account, and a million dollar condo on Chicago's famed Lake Shore Drive.

This was the world Julie created, piece by piece and block by block. It was a world most folks could only dream about. Indeed, it was a world few women entered back when she first began. Yet with all of Julie's success and fame, something was always missing. It was the same something that had been missing for as long as she could remember. The something that had always haunted and driven her to succeed beyond all normal boundaries. The one thing she craved beyond anything else in the world. A sign of recognition for a job well done, from her stepparents/grandparents.

Never once, from the time she was a child until the present, could Julie ever recall either of them offering a word of encouragement or expressing a sense of pride for something she had done. All she ever received was criticism. No matter how much she excelled. It was always the same —"Why didn't you do better?" or "If you had done such and such, you could have won first place, instead of second."— Even now, after having proven herself time and again, nothing ever changed. And it never would. Though it was never said, or even hinted too, and Julie herself did not know, Jennifer and Sir Harry could not accept the fact that their granddaughter was the product of a Jewish mother.

CHAPTER ELEVEN

Gravnick became convinced that funds for the Winton Cosmetics International take-over had to have come from illicit sources. But who, where? When a cursory search by Interpol came up empty-handed, Gravnick decided to spend some of the department's contingency funds. Flying to Zurich, he inserted himself into the middle of the investigation.

The first leg of his flight on Northwest from Chicago landed Gravnick in Amsterdam, where he was to catch a connecting flight on KLM to Zurich. Debarking at Amsterdam's Schiphol Airport, Ernie was struck by the massive contemporary structure that confronted him; one of world's largest and busiest airport facilities.

He had a long lay-over before boarding his KLM flight, so Gravnick took a look around. As he glimpsed the many duty free shops that lined his path, he encountered a group of eager young women who had gathered in apparent anticipation of an arriving passenger. A celebrity perhaps? It mattered not to him. However, as Gravnick began pushing through the crowd, a sudden cacophony of screams arose from the group. Totally out of control they rushed forward to close in on their prey.

Not until some minutes later when safely away from the near riotous scene, Gravnick subconsciously turned in time to spot a familiar figure emerging from amid the chaos. Encircled by an entourage of body guards and personal aides, Julie Winton momentarily materialized. She appeared slightly disheveled but nonetheless beautiful as she strode off.

What the hell is she doing here? The unexpected sight of Julie in Amsterdam immediately had him playing mind games. *She's up to something? Is she more involved in this case than I thought? What could she be covering up? How could she have known I was going to be here in Europe? On the other hand, she is an international celebrity and may well be here on business.*

What's the matter with you, Gravnick? You're getting paranoid over nothing. It's probably a coincidence. What she does is really none of your business.

By the time he arrived in Zurich later in the day, any thoughts of Julie Winton were washed away, if not by disinterest, then from the exhaustion of jet lag.

After clearing Customs and picking up his bag, Ernie made his way through Zurich International, also called Kloten airport due to its location in the town of Kloten. He descended downstairs and entered the airport railway station that lay directly beneath the terminal building. He had been told he could catch a train into the city.

It was a mid-fall day with a rare but bright Alpine sun glistening off nearby mountain tops when Gravnick finally made it to his hotel room. After dropping his bags, his coat, and his shoes in the middle of the room, his body folded like a piece of wet pasta and fell onto the bed in total exhaustion. Sleep did not come easily. Though he dozed fitfully during the flight, he was now over-stimulated by the time change.

An eerie sensation washed over him. It was as if millions of tiny needles were trying to find their way out of his skin. He tried to monitor his breathing. Deep breaths, slow release. Finally, he fell asleep.

When he awakened, Gravnick dragged his body from the bed and headed directly for the combination tub-shower occupying the late 19th century European hotel bathroom.

In the shower, the jet of icy alpine water caught Gravnick completely off guard. As he struggled with the faucet, trying to adjust the temperature, he realized he'd gone to another extreme — the water was now too hot. Then the bedroom telephone began to ring. He ran naked out of the shower and grabbed the phone. "What?"

"Monsieur Gravnick?"

"Who is this?"

"Monsieur Gravnick?" the anxious voice persisted.

"Gravnick here. Who is this?"

"Ah, Monsieur Gravnick. Let me welcome you to Zurich. I am inspector

Jean Caron, here to assist you during your stay in our country. I am presently in the lobby of your hotel and ready to brief you on our investigation. May I come up?"

Gravnick let out an audible moan.

"I beg your pardon, sir." exclaimed Jean Caron.

Looking up, Gravnick saw the absurdity of his situation reflected back from the bureau mirror. He began to laugh at himself.

"If you could see me right now, believe me, sir, you'd understand."

"Ah, yes, I believe I do. Perhaps I have caught you at an inopportune time."

"You might say that, yes. Give me a just few minutes and I'll meet you down in the lobby bar."

At five feet tall and half again as wide, Jean Caron resembled a box with head, arms, legs and feet. But as Gravnick knew from experience, such a man could be like a tank. In this case, a tank with a moustache. Immaculately dressed in dark vested suit, black and white striped shirt and red bow tie, he exemplified the embodiment of a French gentleman. And that was exactly who he was, for he had been born and raised on the Normandy Peninsula and had graduated from the Cherbourg School of Engineering.

Gravnick was quick to put a face to the voice on the phone. Likewise, Caron knew the tall athletic fellow with the easy slouch had to be the American. Rising from the table where he had been waiting, Caron met Gravnick with a frontal pull at the shoulders. With surprising strength, he drew the six-foot-four Gravnick down to his level and kissed him on both cheeks. Gravnick flushed red, barely holding back his distaste. Then he looked away.

Caron was quick to ease the situation. "Ah, Monsieur Gravnick, you are not used to our ways. Do not be embarrassed. Please, won't you join me?"

Within minutes they were relaxed in conversation.

"You'll be interested to know," said Caron, "that upon receiving Interpol's unremarkable report, we began checking our own financial sources. We discovered that beginning several weeks prior to the murder of Monsieur Wilder and the attack upon Madame Wilder, numerous large deposits were made to a variety of new accounts in Zurich, Geneva, and elsewhere. Though the size of these deposits would not be unusual in our country, the fact that of the more than two hundred new customers acquiring accounts during that period, exactly one hundred and fifty of them deposited identical sums of money. Moreover, each account was opened in a different bank, by seemingly unrelated persons, representing a variety of account holders."

"How much money are we talking about?"

"Exactly $77,000,000 American dollars were deposited into each account. Of course when totaled together, we are left with the rather lofty sum of 11.5 billion, an amount that certainly might be considered to buy a controlling interest in a company such as Winton Cosmetics International, Inc."

"Holy Shit, you may have hit the jackpot!"

"Though our verbalization may be a bit less colorful, we are of a similar mind. However, things are a bit more complex than we had hoped for."

"What do you mean? Won't the banks cooperate? I heard Swiss banks were notorious when it comes to getting information from them."

"Well, Monsieur Ernie, that is not so much the problem it formerly was. In recent years our banking laws have made it more possible for authorities to investigate suspected crimes. This came about many years after World War Two, and then only following much international outcry forced the discovery of hordes of ill-gotten treasures that had been secretly stored away by the Nazis during and immediately following the war."

"Yeah, I remember reading something a few years ago. They found art, jewelry and other valuables that had been confiscated from Jews and others throughout Europe during the time of the Holocaust."

"So then what's the problem? Can't we just start tracing the originating source for each of these transactions?"

"Ah, but we already have, only to find the names listed on each account belonged to persons long deceased, and the companies represented, turned out to be fictitious. Furthermore, the funds were wired in one day and out the next, and the accounts henceforth closed."

"Well, then, we'll just have to follow the money to its next destination."

"Yes, but that's not so simple, my friend. You see, the funds were apparently dispersed to multiple locations, with multiple account holders around the world."

"So where do we start?"

"As one of the recipient banks is in Geneva, I suggest that we begin tomorrow with a train ride."

Chapter Twelve

At 5:30 the next morning Gravnick was seated next to Jean Caron on their way to Geneva. Ernie munched a croissant and sipped coffee purchased from the railway's minibar. Caron told him he would wait until 7 a.m., when regular food service would be available.

"I'm looking forward to the ride through the Swiss countryside this morning," Gravnick said.

"I'm afraid you will be somewhat disappointed, my friend. The train we are on is used mostly for commuting between the two cities. It is the shortest route and will take us less than three hours. Unfortunately there is little in the way of beauty to be seen. The surroundings are mostly flat and somewhat boring. To experience the boundless beauty of Switzerland you need follow one of the many other routes, such as the Golden Pass line. Of course it would require more time. If you are able to stay a few extra days or return at another time, I would be honored to escort you."

"Thank you, Jean, I hope someday to take you up on your offer."

"When you come back, be sure to leave time for a few stops and side trips. You will definitely want to spend time in areas like Interlaken and Luzerne, or Montreux and Bern. As for our mission today, I am not certain how much we will actually be able to achieve in Geneva."

"What do you mean?"

"Of course, Switzerland has long been known as the private banking center of the world. The tradition of bank secrecy actually dates back to the middle ages. You might recall in 2008, UBS became embroiled in a controversy that brought in the U.S. FBI, the Department of Justice, and the Security and Exchange Commission. A Swiss bank whistleblower testified to how UBS had its North American sales force recruit U.S. tax payers, and offer them off-shore financial vehicles to hide their assets and evade taxes. The case sparked a lot of pressure on UBS, and on Swiss banks in General. It led to an erosion of Switzerland's fabled bank secrecy laws. But as mentioned, it only applied to certain non-Swiss clients. So, though not quite the tax haven it formerly was, even with proof of a crime, it can still require a court order to break through the secrecy cloak."

"Does that mean they can just refuse to tell us anything with no recourse?"

"Actually, unless we can prove a crime was committed, they could do just that. However, I have had past dealings with the people in charge of the Picket Bank. André Flemn, president of the Picket, is related to my soon-to-be daughter-in-law."

The remainder of the trip passed uneventfully, as the two men discussed strategies on how to best handle the logistics of their upcoming treasure hunt. They arrived on time in Geneva at 8:13 a.m. Caron led his American visitor to a nearby taxi for the short ride to their destination on the Rue Viguet.

Gravnick wondered why the building at number 27 Rue Viguet looked like an ordinary old brown stone residence. He had imagined some kind of magnificent edifice. In reality, there was no indication of a commercial enterprise.

Caron rang the doorbell. Inside a buzzer gave them entrance into a small vestibule. As the door closed behind them, Gravnick was struck by the absurdity of a single light bulb hanging from the ceiling. Then he saw they were surrounded by exposed steel walls. Even the door they just entered was now covered by a steel wall that slid quietly into place.

"When they say private banking, they really mean private," Gravnick quipped.

Then a voice crackled from a hidden speaker asking for identities and purpose of visit. Not until they answered a lengthy series of questions did the wall in front of them silently move aside, exposing a utilitarian waiting room, where they were instantly met by an aide to André Flemn.

Legendary Swiss efficiency, Gravnick mused to himself, as they were led down a short hallway and into the comfortable, but austere office.

André Flemn stepped from behind his desk to greet the two men. He politely pumped Gravnick's hand, hugged Caron in a brief but familiar manner, and without breaking stride, motioned them to a small sofa. As his guests seated themselves, Flemn quickly settled into an opposite wingback chair and waited.

After a moment of silent appraisal, Flemn inquired, "So Jean, what brings you to our humble establishment? I understand from my assistant that it has something to do with a case you are both working on?"

Caron gave a short version of their investigation.

"How can I possibly be of service? As you know our customers expect complete privacy. I don't really see how I can help."

"André, let me tell you what we know. First, we are aware that a rather large sum of money, 77,000,000 American dollars to be exact, was wired into a numbered account at your bank on April 30th. The name on the originating account was Henson Works, Ltd. of Amsterdam, NL. However, this company does not at present, nor ever before show any sign of being in existence. The contact shown on the account has proven to be long deceased. We have further reason to believe that immediately upon receipt, the funds were rewired to a further destination and that account was then closed."

"Well, I must say that the two of you seem to know more of what goes on in my bank than I do. But even if this is true, unless you can show me reason to believe that any of these transactions were part of an illegal scheme, I don't see how I can assist you."

Caron and Gravnick each related the evidence they had uncovered. "We are privy to the fact that, on the very same day said funds were wired to your bank, identical amounts were also wired to numerous accounts in banks around the world. The exact number of those accounts, including the Picket being 150. The number of different banks was also 150. Of the funds destined for those accounts in countries not as secretive as those here in Switzerland, all were immediately wired out to other destinations, and the accounts henceforth closed."

Caron continued —"It doesn't take a genius to guess how the funds in those destination accounts were handled. This is not something a person with honest intentions would do. We are hoping you might be able to help us trace the destination of said funds."

André Flemn rubbed his chin thoughtfully. "If what you say is true, I would certainly have to agree that there may be grounds for suspicion. However, as I am bound to do what I can to protect the privacy of our customers, I will have to insist that you have a court order, before I am able to comply with your request. I am sorry for the inconvenience, gentleman, but you must understand my position."

As if on cue, Flemn abruptly stood up. "Well, gentleman, I must now meet with a very important client." He then walked directly to the door, opened it and walked out, leaving the two men looking dumbfounded at each other.

"Well," said Caron. "I guess that means we need a court order."

"It seems that way," Gravnick said, shaking his head.

On leaving, Gravnick heard a woman's voice that was all too familiar. And there in the reception area stood André Flemm, arm-in-arm with his very important client, Julie Winton.

"Why, Ernie Gravnick. What a nice surprise. But, tell me, what on earth are you doing here?"

"Mrs. Wilder."

"My, we're so formal, aren't we? You always call me Julie. But it's Ms. Winton now. You understand, I want no reminder of that thieving bastard I was married to."

Bowing his head Gravnick replied, "Nice seeing you again *Ms. Winton.*" And then he continued past into the steel-lined vestibule, whereupon the inner metal panel quickly slid closed and the outer panel slid open, allowing them to exit the front door without looking back.

Caron said, "May I ask what that was that all about?"

"I don't trust her. Seeing her at the airport in Amsterdam, might have been a coincidence. But showing up here at Picket Bank — at this particular time — and her apparent connection to André Flemm; I'd say that's one too many coincidences."

"I dare say, it leaves some room for doubt, doesn't it?"

Suddenly a speeding van was headed directly toward where they were standing by the curb. Gravnick pulled Caron from harm's way, but in so doing, both men fell. Surprisingly, Caron jumped up, giving precipitous chase to the offending vehicle. Then, almost as abruptly, he stopped cold, turned around, and with a decided limp, walked back.

"Monsieur Gravnick. Monsieur Gravnick. There was no license plate on the truck, but I was able to spot an unusually shaped dent on the rear door." He quickly sketched a picture of the dent in his pocket notebook.

Gravnick shook his head. "Some country," he mumbled to himself.

The resulting bruise to Caron's left leg proved to be rather slight, due to no more than a glancing blow from the van's bumper. His pant leg apparently had suffered a somewhat more severe insult. Having caught on the van's bumper, the material was torn wide, so as to fully reveal the Frenchman's colorful under drawers. They directly matched the bright red of his bow tie.

"That was definitely no coincidence," Gravnick remarked. "Someone knew we were here, didn't like us snooping around, and was waiting for us."

"I would agree. But, I wonder? Do you think, the lovely lady had anything to do with it?"

"I would think she'd be smarter than to try anything this obvious, but with everything else that's going on, I don't really know."

Pulling out a camera phone, Caron quickly snapped a picture of the drawing on his sketch pad. Then, continuing to manipulate the keys on the phone, he explained, "It's a long shot, but I'm sending out an all points alert on this immediately. Maybe we can spot them before they rid themselves of the van."

"It's worth a try," Ernie said.

While awaiting the train back to Zurich, a call-back to Caron confirmed, "What is believed to be the suspect van has been located, abandoned a few blocks from the Picket Bank." Unfortunately, only a bombed out and burning chassis remained, making any immediate evidence impossible.

CHAPTER THIRTEEN

Gravnick arrived back at his hotel in Zurich at 7 p.m. and dined in his room on a not-so-light dinner of Coquille Saint Jacques, the classic French preparation of scallops in a creamy sauce under a crust of bread. Accompanied by a Caesar salad, he downed it all with a nice bottle of pinot grigio, followed by a molten chocolate soufflé for desert.

After updating his notes, Gravnick retired before ten pm. As he lay there falling asleep, his thoughts wandered to Julie Winton. *What is she up to? Could she really have planned the whole thing? But, if she's so clever, would she have wanted to reveal her relationship with the Picket Bank? On the other hand if she wanted them to see her, to what end….and, the van incident outside the bank — who was behind that?*

Nothing made any sense. He saw her lovely smile. Her gracious beauty…

At midnight the telephone rang.

A woman's voice asked, "Why were you so rude to me at the bank today?"

Not sure if he was dreaming, Gravnick tried shaking the sleep from his head.

"Julie? Is this Julie Winton?" he mumbled into the phone.

"Yes, it's Julie. Was there someone else you snubbed today?"

Still unsure of what was happening, Gravnick mumbled, "Why are you calling in the middle of the night? Is something wrong?"

"Damn right, there's something wrong. You treated me as if you hardly knew me. You embarrassed me in front of a business associate and you expect me not to be pissed? Besides it's only midnight. Are you always so crabby at this time of night?"

"What do you want?"

"I'm here in your hotel lobby and I need to speak with you. Are you going to come down or do you want me to come up?"

"Are you drunk?"

"No, I'm not drunk. I just need to talk to you."

"Can't this wait until tomorrow?"

"No, it can't wait — and I can't talk about it here on the phone. Since you apparently don't feel like coming down, I'll come up. What's your room number?"

"Don't come up here."

"Why, Mr. Gravnick, I do believe you're embarrassed at the thought of having a woman visit your room. How quaint," she said.

"That's not it."

"Then why can't I come up?" she said, continuing to tease.

"Because I'm a cop investigating a case that concerns you. It's not right."

"Ernie, dear, you still think I'm a big bad ogre, don't you? You imagine I'm going to bewitch you in some way."

Gravnick sighed. Then he gave her his room number.

"See, that didn't hurt did it?"

He said nothing.

Julie laughed. "Be right up."

Moments later, Gravnick heard a gentle knock. It had to be Julie, but he asked anyway. "Who is it?"

"Attila the Hun, I've come to attack you. Open up."

Gravnick opened the door. Seeing him standing there in his robe, bare-legged and bleary-eyed, Julie reached out, backed him into the room, and kicked the door shut behind her. Looking down, she remarked, "Nice legs."

He shook his head. "What's your problem?"

"What's your problem?" she asked pointedly.

Gravnick, now fully awake said, "Look lady, You've got some nerve. Barging in here — getting me out of bed for no good reason." He hesitated, then said, "I think you're more involved in this thing than you'd like people to think."

"Involved in what thing?"

"The murder of your husband, the attempted takeover of Winton Industries, the whole ball of wax."

"What makes you believe so?"

"Just about everything, from your too perfectly detailed testimony in court, the timing of your trip to Zurich, coincidental to my arrival and layover at Shiphole. Your questionable appearance at the Picket Bank, smack dab in the middle of our meeting. Not to mention, your obvious friendship with André Flemm. Of course, you know nothing about the attempt on Jean Caron's and my life as we left the bank? And, here you are in my room, at this ridiculous hour of the night, acting like a spoiled child. All of this, so soon after, what had to be the most devastating trauma of your life. What else am I to believe?"

"Attempt on your life? What are you talking about?"

"Like you don't know what happened?"

Julie said, "Could we sit down?"

They moved to the comfortable couch.

When Gravnick finished relating the details of Andre's and his narrow escape outside the Picket, Julie seemed genuinely upset. So much so, a tear ran down her cheek marring her meticulous makeup. "I'm so sorry Ernie, you really believe all this was of my doing, don't you?" She shook her head. "You've got to believe me. None of this was planned — at least by me. I can understand your suspicions — all the coincidences. It's like someone set this up to make me look evil. But, really — I've had nothing to do with any of it."

Wiping her tears with the palm of her hand, she said softly, "What do I have to do to convince you that I'm not lying?"

Gravnick stood up and got her a tissue. But when he offered it to her, she took his hand and squeezed it. He responded by sitting next to her and hugging her. They kissed and her tongue found his.

The wake-up call he had left with the front desk came through at 6:00 the next morning and shook him from a soothing sleep. He sat up and his eyes quickly fell upon Julie's clothing piled on the floor, partially covered by the robe and briefs she'd helped him discard the night before.

When he heard the shower running in the bathroom, Gravnick plopped back down in the bed, a smile of contentment on his face. Lost in memories of last night's love-making, he was oblivious that the splashing shower had stopped. Julie appeared with a towel around her waist. This she impulsively flipped open so that it fell at her feet. "Good morning," she said as she slid back into bed next to Gravnick." Afterward, Julie remarked, "What a nice way to begin a day."

Suddenly, breaking from his embrace, Julie jumped up, hastily moved across the room to retrieve her cell phone, and began dialing.

"What are you doing?" Gravnick asked.

She held up her hand and began speaking into the phone:

"It's me. Be a doll and pick up my bags from the hotel. I'll hop a cab and meet you and the others in front of the Kloten Terminal in an hour. Oh, and call Ben. Tell him I'll be doing the show live in New York tonight."

Finishing her call, Julie gathered her clothes and started dressing.

"You're leaving?"

"Yes, I have to be in New York for my show tonight."

"But you said you'd arranged for them to rerun a prior show tonight?"

"Changed my mind. I'm going to do it live." She put on her panties.

Gravnick stared at her tense, perfect nipples. "This isn't fair," he whispered.

In a matter of minutes, Julie threw him a kiss and was half out the door when he said,

"Hey, when will I see you?"

She gave him a wink and a flutter of a finger wave.

Gravnick got up to dress for his morning meeting with Caron. He could still taste her lipstick from the night before.

In fast order, Gravnick completed his shower, dressed and left. Halfway through the hotel lobby, he was greeted by the concierge, who handed him a message. It was from Caron, saying that he was eagerly awaiting him — that upon his return yesterday, he had come across some promising new information. Apparently, he had uncovered something previously unknown in the Thornton Wilder case.

Twenty minutes later, as Gravnick stepped from his taxi across from the Zurich Bureau of Police, the world suddenly began to unravel. At first a trembling sound emerged from what seemed a distance away. Turning slowly in the direction of the disturbance, Gravnick was shaken by a kind of wild cosmic dream.

As in a slow motion movie, the entire front of the building on the other side of the street seemed to come apart piece by piece. Then, at first floating, then crumbling, the building erupted into flying red bricks. The intensity of the explosion forced Gravnick's hands over his ears. The aftershock came next — a violent implosion of everything around, above, and below. Gravnick was slammed to the ground.

Dazed, he tried to sit up only to fall back. After a few minutes, as he regained his bearings, Ernie became aware that the building across the street, where he was to meet Caron, had turned into a heap of fire and rubble.

Another explosion. This one erupted in his head. He realized that the little square man, whom he had grown to like in one day, was in the midst of this devastation. Could he possibly have survived?

As his mind raced, a strange vision began to appear from deep inside the smoke and flaming rubble. At first it seemed an apparition. A glowing outline of a great two-legged beast. A ghoulish flaming specter inched forward, purposely revealing itself, like a phantom rising straight out of the bowels of hell. Then, a desperate blood chilling scream. The apparition before him was the remnant of the man known as "The Tank." Gravnick ran toward him as Jean Caron stumbled and fell, his arms folded around a box.

Gravnick understood the impossibility of what Caron had just accomplished. His skin literally dissolving and falling from his bones…had not prevented him from his final quest to bring the box to him. Gravnick knew that as long as he lived, he would never again know a man like Jean Caron.

CHAPTER FOURTEEN

Gravnick turned away and slowly walked toward the street. A taxi pulled up. Appearing to notice the devastation for the first time, the cabby jumped out and called to Gravnick. "Are you all right? Can I help you?"

Gravnick clutched Caron's parting gift. He half nodded to the cabby who guided him into the back seat of the taxi.

The driver bombarded Ernie with questions. "What happened? Were you inside that building when it blew up? Were the police?"

"As far as I could tell they were in the building," Gravnick said. Then he directed the driver to his hotel and began to examine the metal box Caron had given his life for. It was shut tight with a special lock. He'd need tools.

Gravnick contemplated the events that had occurred since his arrival in Zurich. *The unexpected sighting of Julie Winton at Amsterdam's Shiphole Airport at the time he arrived. His introductory encounter with Jean Caron in the lobby bar of his hotel in Zurich. The effortless manner with which the strange little man put him at ease. Their sojourn to Geneva and their meeting at the Picket Bank with André Flemn. The surprise encounter with Julie Winton in the vestibule of the Picket, and their near fatal run-in with the van outside the bank.*

Suddenly the cab made a sharp turn. Breaks squealed and the vehicle pulled up hard. Gravnick flew head-first into the back of the front seat. Stunned, he tried to get up when the cab driver pulled the door open and began beating him with a baseball bat. Gravnick grabbed for the weapon only to have his hands bludgeoned. A hard blow to the skull knocked him out.

—◦)◦—

Darkness

Silence

Nothingness

A spot of light

Darkness

Silence

Nothingness

Light

A flood of brightness burst forth in a blinding array of whites and yellows. Easing. A face seemed to form, floated in the middle of nowhere. A beautiful face. A woman's face. A familiar face.

No. It can't be. It looks like Julie. Julie Winton. But, she's in New York? Where am I? I can't see anything beyond that face. Hello. Julie, is that you? No answer. *Shit, what am I doing? Am I dreaming? Wow. This is crazy. Got to wake up.*

"Ernie. It's me, Julie. I don't know if you can hear me?"

Stop shouting, I'm not deaf. Of course I can hear you. What are you doing here? You're supposed to be in New York?

"Oh, my sweet Ernie, they said you're in a coma. You really can't hear me can you?"

Coma, what the hell are you talking about? I hear every word you're saying.

Leaning over the bed, Julie bent down and kissed his cheek. She held his bandaged hand.

Now what, I can see you're holding my hand, but I don't feel anything…and what's that bandage on my hand? What is this place? Why don't you answer me?

A door opened. Another voice.

"How's our patient doing?"

"I'm not sure. His eyes look clearer to me," Julie answered. "Sometimes, they seem to look around, as if asking a question. At other times, I could swear he's glaring at me — as if he's really angry — which knowing him, makes me think he hears everything."

"It's very possible. We just don't know. Some coma patients seem to show a sense of awareness and others show nothing."

"I can't remember anything that happened during the entire time when I was comatose."

"As I said, we really don't know. Every patient reacts differently."

Gravnick now sensed that the second voice belonged to a nurse. *Yes, there she is, right beside Julie. Cute little thing.*

Placing a thermometer in his mouth the nurse said, "Let's see what your temperature is today, Mr. Gravnick."

Boiling. Yours would be too if you were in here with me. Ooh. What a nice thought. Come on in. I'll make that pretty little body of yours nice and hot.

The nurse extracted the thermometer. "Temperature's normal."

"When might he come out of the coma?" Julie asked.

"Days, weeks, it's anyone's guess."

Opening the door she asked, "Would you mind stepping out for a few moments? I need to change him."

"No problem."

With that, the nurse pulled the blanket to the bottom of the bed, leaned over and pulled up Gravnick's hospital gown.

"Let's see what you've got there, Mr. Gravnick."

I've a feeling it's not what I'd like you to be interested in.

"Oh. You did real good, but let's get you cleaned up," the nurse said. She picked up his legs like a baby and proceeded to wash his bottom with a cloth.

Tell me this isn't happening.

The nurse finished up and walked out of Gravnick's sight. He heard her open the door and say, "You can come back in now, Miss Winton." There was a rustling, starchy sound as the nurse left.

"Nurse Fletcher told me you were a good boy — that you're all cleaned up and ready for sleep."

Great, now my bowel movements are a topic for public discussion. I suppose if we turned on the evening news, the breaking story would be: 'Gravnick Shits.' Or, better still: 'Gravnick, No Longer, Full of Shit.' What about debating the size of my penis? That would give everyone a good laugh.

As he glanced up at Julie, she whispered softly. "I wonder what is really going on in that head of yours? I can only imagine." Turning away she slipped off her suit jacket and said, "It's been a long day. I guess I might as well turn in for the night myself." Gravnick blinked as Julie stood next to the bed, bent down and planted a soft, wet kiss on his lips. "Good night my love." With that, she stepped back and slowly removed her clothes. If she'd been any slower, he would have been healed and on his way. There she stood, perfectly blond and naked. Then she donned her robe and Gravnick heard the apparent crackling of leather, as Julie turned out the light and settled in the chair. The last thing he heard before falling asleep was Julie's breathing and the beating of his heart.

Julie was awakened by the sound of shouting. The room remained dark except for the light from the hall. She froze as she recognized one of the voices. Gravnick's.

"What the hell are you doing?" Get away from me."

"Mr. Gravnick, I'm Elsa, the night nurse. I need to check your vitals."

"It's the middle of the goddamn night, lady. My vitals are just fine."

Then with a wide sweep of a bandaged arm, he shoved the nurse aside and shouted.

"Get the hell away from me and let me sleep."

Excited to hear Gravnick speaking, Julie jumped up and went to the side of his bed.

"Oh, Ernie, you're back with us. You're speaking. You're moving. Oh my darling. Thank you, Lord, thank you so much."

"Oh, for God's sake. Now you."

The remainder of the night Gravnick slept like a baby

As the sun showed through the window, Julie awakened. She sat back in the chair and began stretching out of the cramped position she had maintained most of the night. Every bone in her body ached. She was going to need a good workout and a massage today. Julie discarded the robe and put on her bra and panties. Then she did her usual morning yoga stretches.

At 6:00 in the morning, the nurse burst into Gravnick's room with a cheer-ful "Good morning!" And then a false, "How's our patient today?" Greeted by the sight of Gravnick's empty bed and Julie sprawled before her on the floor, in an apparent meditative trance — she began rattling off a series of questions.

"What's going on here? Where's the patient? Mr. Gravnick?" Ms. Winton, why are you on the floor like that?"

With no immediate response from Julie, who for the moment remained in a relaxed, deep yoga trance, the nurse fired off another round of questions. "Miss Winton, please explain yourself immediately. What the devil did you do with

Mr. Gravnick? If you don't get up off the floor and tell me where the patient is, I'm going to call security."

From the other side of the partly closed bathroom door, a growl erupted. "What in hell is going on out there? Can't a man take a crap without World War III breaking out?"

Suddenly jumping up from her yoga position, Julie shouted. "What's happening? Where's Gravnick?"

A sudden flushing sound, and Gravnick came out of the bathroom. His bandaged and braced right arm was straight in front of him. He wobbled unsteadily up to the two women. "Help," he said in a mocking voice. The two women got him back in bed. The remainder of the morning turned into a question and answer session.

All the pent-up wondering that had been boxed inside Ernie's head came spewing forth in an avalanche of why, when, who and how?

CHAPTER FIFTEEN

"Where am I? How did I get here? It's not Switzerland — English — too good. The department — do they know? How did I get so banged up? Mother…did anyone contact my mother? How long have I been here?"

"If you shut up for a moment, I'll tell you."

Gravnick fell silent and listened as Julie related how he'd been found in a gutter several blocks from the bombed-out Zurich Police Headquarters. "They thought you were dead — then discovered you were alive — but in a deep coma. They got you to a hospital."

"How did you find out?" Gravnick asked.

"That night after my show in New York, I decided to call and apologize for the abrupt way I walked out on you. The hotel clerk told me you weren't in your room, or at least you were not answering your phone. So, I hung up and figured to catch up with you next day."

"Then what?"

"Something kept on gnawing at me. Knowing how you are with getting your sleep, I called back. After the desk tried your room again to no avail, I asked to speak to the doorman and the concierge. Both confirmed you'd not returned to the hotel."

"So how did you find out where I was?"

"Knowing that you were working with the local constabulary, my next call was to the Zurich Police. I received a recorded message explaining that, due to the bombing of the police headquarters building, a state-of-emergency had been declared — all police business was being handled by the military command."

"I kind of remember saying something to the cabbie — the police — all dead," Gravnick muttered."

"After hearing the message, danger signals began flashing in my head. I had to know where you were — if you were involved in the bombing — if so — were you all right. It took me three more calls. This time to Zurich Hospitals. After much waiting — screaming — and telling a little white lie — like I was your wife — when asked if I was immediate family, I was told that you had been brought in to the Universitats Spital — a local hospital."

"How long was I there?"

"They kept you for tests and observation for almost two weeks. They had to make certain your vital signs remained steady and you were okay to be moved."

"So how did I get here? And where is here?"

"You're in the North Shore Healthcare facility in Highland Park. After discussions with your office and your mother, I arranged for a private jet and medical staff to have you transported back to Chicago. Upon landing at O'Hare you were immediately picked up by ambulance and brought here. You've been in a coma for the past three and a half weeks, until suddenly waking last night."

Showing displeasure, Gravnick questioned, "You contacted my mother? How did—" Julie interrupted mid-sentence. "Your office told me your mother was listed as next of kin and I needed to get her permission to move you — and before you go off on me — I found your mother to be a very special lady. She is a lot stronger than you seem to realize."

"What do you know about my mother? How dare you tell me —"

"Because I assumed she'd be worried about you — I've visited with her several times since you arrived back. It has been an honor to get to know her. She's a very warm and caring person who absolutely idolizes you, you big oaf."

"Just who did you tell her you are? And what is our relationship supposed to be?"

"I told her exactly who I am — how we met and how we ran into each other in Zurich."

"Yeah, and what else did you say?"

"Oh, she just loved the part about how I attacked you in your hotel room and forced you to have sex with me." She hesitated as Ernie sat quietly with his mouth open. "Seriously, she did ask if we had slept together."

"And I suppose you said yes?"

"I told her that was a question she would need to ask you."

Gravnick said, "And, believe me — she will."

—◌◦◦—

Over the next few weeks in the hospital, Gravnick immersed himself in physical therapy, working overtime re-learning to walk rather than drag his legs one at a time. He also spent an inordinate amount of time with finger and arm exercises, to get dexterity and movement back. They had been so badly bashed and broken from the beating he had undergone.

Meanwhile, Julie, who had taken a partial leave from her everyday business duties, began alternating her time from office to hospital. She also continued to cover Gravnick's Sunday visits with his mother, which aggravated him no end.

Before his release from the hospital, Gravnick's doctor said that he would need out-patient therapy for several weeks, perhaps months, for his limbs to regain total movement.

"You will also need to get someone to help you get around and care for you — and don't try walking up or down stairs on your own."

Gravnick argued that he'd be fine on his own. "As for stairs, I live in a second-floor walkup apartment, and I need to get back to work."

Julie said, "I believe I have an idea that just might work. Realizing that Mr. Gravnick may require a transition plan, I was going to suggest he temporarily move into the new house my son Jonathan and I recently acquired. He could have his own room on the first floor, which by the way, is adjacent to a fully equipped gym that could be useful in his therapy program. I have also taken the liberty of checking out the availability of an aide to assist him and found a very reliable service."

Laughing, Gravnick answered, "Miss Winton, you are really something. Do you believe I would fall for something so obvious?"

"Why not?" Julie asked. "We've got the space and the perfect set-up. Not only that, you'd be a lot closer to your office. That is, once you're able to spend a few hours back at work."

"Come on, lady. Give me a little credit. Aside from a few hundred other reasons, you still happen to be a suspect — and not just any suspect, but after everything that went down in Zurich, my number one suspect. There is just no way I'm going to move into your place. That would be like knowingly crawling into the spider's web."

"So what are you going to do?"

"I'll get along just fine. I'll get someone to help me up and down stairs at the apartment and to do some shopping and even drive me to the office."

"I can just picture you letting some big lug of an aide apply a hospital carry to you — your arms around his neck — your face in his — as he hauls you up and down two flights of steps — with your neighbors looking on in anticipation. What a sight that would make. Furthermore, I have to tell you your suspicion of me as public enemy number one is completely flawed," said Julie.

"What do you mean flawed?"

"Look, if I really wanted you out of the way, why on earth would I have gone to all the effort and expense of having you brought back to the States? It would have been so much simpler to have had you taken out while you were still over there. It would also have given me the perfect alibi — 'I was in New York doing a live TV show at the time.' Another thing, if your great powers of deduction were being applied properly, you would have realized that whoever is after you doesn't really want you dead. To the contrary, it seems they have gone out of their way to interject every stumbling block they can come up with to discourage you. Even with this last episode, which I'll admit probably got a little out of hand, you were left in a coma, not dead."

"So, now you're suddenly the detective? You don't know what you're talking about. They sure weren't trying to protect me when they blew up the police headquarters building."

"What makes you think they had any idea you were going to be there?" said Julie.

"How could anyone have known? Did you tell someone? Was it advertised somewhere? Maybe a billboard exclaiming 'Super sleuth Chief of Detectives Ernest Gravnick is in town.' Did you ever stop to think that maybe it was your friend, Jean Caron, the bad guys were after — that perhaps they were worried he had stumbled onto information that could be harmful to them — and took him out to prevent his passing it on to you? You've got to admit it's possible."

"Sure, it's possible, but it's not necessarily the only answer. I could have mentioned to you that I was meeting Caron that morning."

"You could have, but you didn't. And even if you had, when did I have the time or opportunity to set up such an elaborate operation? The only phone call I made that morning was right in front of you, telling my manager to meet me at the airport and call my TV producer regarding the show in New York that night."

"Well, your call could have contained a coded message…"

"Come on, Ernie. Even if I'd somehow concocted a secret message through my phone call, it would have taken a lot more than — what was it — an hour, hour a half at most between the time of my call and the time the place blew up?"

"Yeah, well, I guess maybe you're right. Now that I think of it, that cabbie was just sitting there waiting. It's for sure he was involved with whoever blew up the place. He was probably there to make sure no one got out alive. When he saw me pick up the box Caron had, it's no wonder he became anxious to help me. He needed to keep me from seeing its contents."

"Okay, now that you're finally thinking straight, may I ask again whether you'll at least consider my offer?"

"What offer?"

"Oh, Jesus, Gravnick, sometimes you are so dense. I'm asking you to consider moving into my place while you're recovering."

"I guess it makes some sense. I suppose I could consider it. But don't think it's anywhere near a done deal. I need some time to think it over. And, by the way, don't feel you're entirely off the hook. I still have a lot of questions for you."

"I'd be very disappointed if you weren't interested in me, Mr. Gravnick."

That night as Ernie fell asleep, he thought about what Julie said.

Did someone find out Caron had uncovered damaging information and took him out by blowing up the Zurich Police Headquarters? But how? Who was it, who? Could it have been an inside job? I'll have Dilly put together a list of suspects, and get Interpol to do the same.

CHAPTER SIXTEEN

Three days later Gravnick was told that he was being released from the hospital. As an aide wheeled him in a chair through the automatic sliding doors to the patient pickup area, a stretch limousine pulled up in front of him. The front passenger door opened and Gravnick was confronted by a behemoth of a man. The giant extended his hand and spoke softly. "Chief Gravnick? I'm Sampson, and I'll be helping you for the next few weeks."

So there he was at Julie's new estate in Highland Park, Bella Vista. He and Sampson quickly became friends. Gravnick discovered that as a young man, Sampson had enlisted in the Marines, where he served as an MP. Following his release from the Corps, he'd also Done a stint as an investigator for a PI firm. That was prior to returning to school, where he earned degrees in nursing and physical therapy. Ernie found the big man surprisingly gentle, with a great sense of humor, and a curious mind. And Sampson was drawn to Gravnick in the same way Gravnick was drawn to him.

That evening, as Sampson wheeled him into the dining room for dinner, he saw Jonathan for the first time since the young man turned fourteen. "Chief Gravnick, I didn't know you were here. I thought you'd arrive later this evening. I've been working in my dark room since I came home from school, and didn't hear you come in. Please accept my apology for not being here to greet you and show you around."

"Jonathan, good to see you. Sampson and I have been exploring on our own. This place is truly beautiful."

"Thank you. Mother and I are very pleased with it."

"I don't believe you've met Sampson. He'll be helping me out for a while."

"Mr. Sampson, good to meet you sir," Jonathan said.

"Sampson's my first name. Sampson Bielegowski, to be exact. But everyone calls me by my first name. Okay with you?"

"Yes sir, that's good," the boy replied — immediately adding, "Oh, Chief, did you get the message that Mother had a last minute meeting? She won't be able to join us for dinner."

"I hadn't heard. But that will give us a chance to get to know each other better."

By the time they finished eating dinner, Gravnick discovered that both Sampson and Jonathan were pretty good chess players — Sampson, picked up the game in the service, while Jonathan learned on the internet.

When Julie arrived home later in the evening, she found the three of them out on the patio, with Jonathan apparently having the upper hand in a game with Gravnick, while Sampson looked on in amusement.

After breakfast on Sunday, Julie asked Sampson to bring Gravnick out front, where her car was waiting to take them to the Deerfield nursing home, to visit his mother. When they arrived outside the door to Dora's room, Gravnick abruptly pulled the break on his wheel chair. He turned to Sampson and Julie and began to rise up from the chair. Supported half on the arm of his chair and half against the door frame, Gravnick insisted, "I'm not letting my mother see me this way."

Julie pulled two collapsible canes from her handbag. Handing them to Gravnick, she smiled. Then said, "Stubborn."

Dora's first glance at Gravnick, as he leaned heavily on the two canes in her doorway, brought an immediate look of dismay. Then seeing Julie, she smiled.

"Well, I see you finally listened to me and got yourself a pretty girl to spend time with. Smells good too, doesn't she? A hell of a lot better than this place, eh? And what the hell did you go and do, to get yourself all broken up like that? Don't just stand there staring at me like some kind of an idiot. Come give your decrepit old mother a hug."

Gravnick struggled across the room to where Dora sat in a wheelchair. He gripped the canes and gave her a kiss. He righted himself and gave her the same rough treatment she'd given him. "I see you haven't changed a bit, you old wind bag, and before you ask whether I've slept with Julie, it's none of your business."

"Ah, I knew it. You didn't have to tell me. The second I laid eyes on her, I said, 'He's having his way with this one.' Bet she really ruffles your comforter, doesn't she?"

Gravnick shook his head. "Same old, same old."

Dora smiled at Julie. "How are you doin', honey? Who's the hunk standing there with you? I sure could go for a piece of that."

"Sampson, this is Dora. In case you haven't figured it out yet," Julie said, laughing.

"Nice to meet you, Mrs. Gravnick," Sampson said.

"Don't be so sure about that, young man. I can be a real pain in the ass."

"Yes, Ma'am."

Gravnick said, "Sampson's helping me while I heal."

"I imagine there's a story on that score. Who did you bust up to get so twisted up?"

"You should see the other guy."

Chapter Seventeen

O ver the next several weeks Gravnick's days were taken up by hours of physical therapy. They were also mixed with phone meetings with Jack Dilly, who had taken over in his absence. His routine included some serious chess with Sampson and Jonathan, who seemed to be enjoying their time with Gravnick.

Whether playing chess or sitting around talking, Gravnick noticed the boy was often seeking him out. But it wasn't until Jonathan invited him to view his new photography project that Gravnick realized the boy was leaning towards a father figure he never really had. Julie had mentioned that Jonathan's darkroom was off limits to anyone outside of herself.

So, Gravnick being invited in was an indication that the boy's acceptance was growing. His time with Julie followed a normal family pattern of evenings and weekends. More and more Bella Vista was a comfort zone for Gravnick, but as his therapy sessions tapered off, he began to spend daylight hours at his office.

"It sure is good to have you back around here," Dilly told him. "With the case load that's piled up, I need all the help I can get."

"Don't forget I'm still recovering, only here part-time," Gravnick said. "You're still the one in charge."

"Yeah, yeah, I know, Boss," Dilly said.

"So what have you got for me?"

Slamming a pile of files on the table, Dilly said, "This ought to keep you out of my hair for a while."

Though the Winton/Wilder case remained uppermost with Gravnick, there were plenty of other cases that also took precedence.

Gravnick asked Sampson, "Want to help me out with some research?"

"Sounds good," Sampson answered. "It's pretty boring staring at the back of your head."

Gravnick shoved half of his recent files over to Sampson.

Thumbing through the remaining files, Gravnick's attention was drawn to a hit and run case. The incident occurred on Saturday night around midnight at the corner of Green Bay Road and Park Avenue West, in downtown Highland Park. According to a witness, the victim, a 25-year-old Northwestern University grad student, identified as a Jennifer Russo of nearby Highwood, had been run down by a dark color, late model Mercedes sedan. "The driver — the witness thought it was a man — never slowed down or hesitated after hitting the woman. "It was as if it he meant to hit her."

Suddenly, Gravnick began shouting to Sampson, as if the big man were in another room, instead of sitting across from him. "I need you to get on the phone and start calling Mercedes dealers and high-end body shops within a 50 mile area, for any recent model, dark colored Mercedes, brought in with front-end damage since Saturday night. Maybe we'll get lucky. Meanwhile, I'll contact Motor Vehicle for a list of recent model Mercedes owner's in the same metro."

Sampson was surprised by the number of automobile body shops in the phone book.

"This is going to take weeks.."

"You want to do cop work?" Gravnick challenged.

Sampson shrugged, continued making calls. By the time he completed a dozen or so calls, a computer readout from Motor Vehicle surprised Gravnick.

"Sal-va-tore Gia-conte, Jr. I'll be a son-of-a-bitch."

"Who's he?" Sampson asked.

"The son of the man I tried to put away for the murder of my father and my grandfather, Caesar Casilone — and then, only being able to nail him on the lesser charges of money laundering and fraud. Junior was a kid the last time I saw him. But it looks like he might not have fallen too far from the family tree."

"Also, back in the day when I was a cop burning shoe leather, I interviewed a witness by the name of Anthony Russo. The encounter had taken place at the man's home on Kedzie Avenue, on Chicago's southwest side. Russo was friendly — invited me into his kitchen for a cup of coffee. While we spoke, his daughter, who was then about three or four years old, kept running in and out of the room. The more Russo tried to quiet her down, the more she ran around, laughing and teasing, as little girls of that age do. I told her I was a policeman and wanted her to guard the kitchen door. After that she quieted down. Her name, come to think, was Jennifer…Jennifer Russo. The same name as the woman who was run down and killed this past Saturday night." Gravnick thought a moment — *two names from the past.*

"Grab your coat. We're out-a-here."

"I've still got a load of calls to finish up."

"Forget them. We're going to pay a visit on Mr. Giaconte Jr. Besides, this guy would never take his car to a legit body shop. Most likely he'd have ditched it at a chop-shop. By now it's long gone."

Next Gravnick placed a call to his old friend Charley House with the Chicago police. The voice at the other end answered, "Captain House."

"Well if it isn't Charley Horse, as we used to say. How the hell are you?"

"Oh, shit, Gravnick. When are you going to grow up?"

"I don't have to tell you that. You know the answer."

"Yeah. Never. So what's on your mind? You wouldn't be calling unless you needed something."

"Still mean as a teased snake, aren't you? So, I'd like to borrow an officer for a couple hours to pay a visit on a suspected hit and run perp, who happens to live in your town."

"This about the hit and run in the Sunday *Trib*?"

" Yeah, looks like Giaconte's kid may be involved."

"Christ. That's all we need, you churning up another media circus in town. All right. Give me the address. I'll have a man meet you there…about forty-five minutes."

"That should work. Thanks, Charley Horse."

After checking with Dilly, he and Sampson took off for Junior's house.

"Aren't you supposed to be working part time," Sampson asked.

"For me, this is part time," Gravnick replied.

Later, turning onto Giaconte's street, they saw a city cop getting out of a parked squad car a few doors down. It took but one ring of the doorbell for Junior to answer, as if he was expecting them. "Chief Gravnick." Junior said. "What brings you to our city?"

"Like to ask you a few questions, Sal. Mind if we come in?"

"Not at all, come in." They made themselves uncomfortable, as Gravnick liked to say, in Giaconte's garish living room.

"First off, tell us what you know about Jennifer Russo?"

"Never heard of her. What'd she do?"

"I'll ask the questions," Gravnick said.

Giaconte nodded.

"Now, then, where were you this past Saturday night?"

Hesitating a moment, Giaconte looked vaguely around the room. "Saturday. Oh, yeah. Came home after dinner and stayed in all night."

"Did anyone see you, who might be able to vouch for your being here?"

"Come on. What's this all about?"

"I told you, I'll ask the questions."

"Okay, there was woman with me. Picked her up at a bar — she stayed the night. End of story."

"I don't suppose she had a name?" Gravnick asked.

"Rose, I think. You know how it is."

"No, I don't know how it is. Why don't you tell me? How about the name of the bar?"

"I had a lot to drink. I think it might have been on Halsted St., in Old Town."

"You're certain you were home all night? No possible way you might have been in Highland Park, say, around midnight? Maybe driving in the area of Green Bay Road. and Park Avenue West?"

"I told you, I was here all night."

"I only have a few more questions."

"Okay. Shoot."

"You own a dark color, late model, four door Mercedes?"

"Ah, that's what this is all about. You're here about my stolen car. Did you find it?"

Showing no reaction, Gravnick replied, "Not really. Why don't you tell us about it."

"You don't know, do you? I called in a report the other day. The car was gone Sunday morning when I went to take the girl home."

"Interesting — and how'd the girl get home?"

"Called a cab."

"Was that before or after you called the police about the car?"

"I believe it was before. I didn't want her to have to wait around, so I called the cab company first and then I called the police."

"You wouldn't happen to remember what cab company you called, would you?"

"Probably a Yellow, but I'm not sure. You know, I was pretty upset.

That vehicle cost me a pretty bundle. I just opened the phone book to Cabs, and called the first number I saw."

"Are you sure the heading was Cabs, not Taxis?"

"What kind of a question is that?"

"Humor me, okay?"

"Well, I'm not sure. I guess it could have been Taxis."

"You guess it could have been Taxis? In other words you don't know?"

"Like I said, I was pretty shook up. Anyway, Cabs, Taxis, what is the difference?"

Gravnick nodded and he and Sampson headed for the front door. Looking back, Gravnick offered one last remark. "Hey, for your information, Sal, there is no heading for Cabs in the *Chicago Phone Directory,* only Taxis."

Out on the sidewalk, Ernie said, "The kid's lying through his teeth. He's as guilty as they come. But we need a lot more than we have." Knowing it might be a waste of time, Gravnick had Sampson drive him over to Chicago's near-north side, where they spend the remainder of the day checking out the bar and lounge scene on N. Halted St. Of course no one remembered seeing anyone of Giaconte's description.

On the way back to Bella Vista later in the day, Gravnick made a call to check out the stolen vehicle report on Giaconte's car. He found that Giaconte had indeed filed a report early Sunday morning just as he said.

"Disproves nothing," Gravnick said to Sampson. "He could have been driving the car at the time of the incident and still have had plenty of time to ditch the vehicle, get home, and call in the report. We're going to have to dig further on this one."

A moment later Gravnick added, "You know, if my scenario's right, he needed a way home. Likely, he took a cab from the chop shop; and if so, the cab company would have a record. Check that out, Sampson".

CHAPTER EIGHTEEN

After pulling through the gate into the secluded driveway leading to Bella Vista, Sampson saw Julie's limo approaching in the rearview mirror. As it turned in behind them it came to a brief stop, waiting for the automatic gate to re-open. Before the limo was able to continue its journey through the gate, the quietness of the late suburban afternoon was abruptly shattered by the pounding of automatic weapon fire.

After a screeching halt, Sampson shouted to Gravnick, "Get out!" then slid from the car, and lay flat on his belly. As the black Cadillac slowly pulled away, Gravnick ran towards Julie's bullet-riddled limo — its ear-splitting air horns piercing. Gravnick saw the bloodied body of Dylan Sullivan, Julie's long time chauffeur and body guard, slumped across steering wheel, his shoulder jamming the horn.

He tried the door — locked.

Julie Winton's body was curled on the floor. "Julie" he shouted, pounding on the window, but there was no movement.

Breathless, Sampson appeared.

"Sampson, I can't get in here. Try the doors on the other side."

"They're locked too," Sampson yelled. "We'll have to break a window."

Sampson stooped, plucked a rock from the edge of the driveway, and punched through the safety glass, pushed the crumpled window in, and unlocked the door.

A trickle of blood ran down Julie's forehead. Gravnick let out a cry.

The air horns were still blasting as Sampson pulled Dylan Sullivan from the horn. He put an index and forefinger to Sullivan's neck. "He's gone".

Gravnick lowered his face to Julie's, and felt her warm, sweet breath. "She's alive," he said, and took in every feature of Julie's lovely face. Even though there was a mixture of makeup, mascara and dirt-not to mention blood-Gravnick thought, *I've never seen anything quite so beautiful in my life.*

Moments later the EMT's arrived. They found that Julie had a quarter inch deep bullet wound on the crown of her skull. "Fortunately," the EMT said, "it's a graze, an indirect bullet abrasion."

As he looked at her, a single tear fell from Gravnick's eye and landed in the middle of Julie's forehead. She blinked, and rubbed her eyes. Gravnick told her the EMTs would be taking care of her. "I've no intention of going to the hospital. Just bandage me up so I can go home."

"No way," the EMT told her. "You've undergone severe shock, and you're going to need several stiches on your head."

The doctors will want to keep you overnight for observation," the second EMT added.

"Okay, but, only if you'll go with me, Gravnick."

"I'll follow right behind, Okay?"

"I guess," Julie said.

Jack Dilly showed up and Gravnick brought him up to date on what happened. "Does this shit have no end?" Dilly said. "I mean, who the hell …"

On the way to the hospital, Gravnick told Sampson, "It could be related to the situation involving the takeover attempt of her company's stock, the murder of her husband, and the nasty aftermath that followed. We still haven't solved that case. And, we really don't have that much to go on. I just don't know."

"What else could it be?" Sampson asked.

"Could be someone's trying to threaten me, to scare me off. Like those times in Europe. But it's been a few months since all that went down. Plus, I've been out of commission, unable to do much in the way of follow up. It doesn't make sense that anyone would want to stir things up when nothing's been happening. Most folks don't even know that I'm back among the living…" Then he added, suddenly, "Except that little son-of-a-bitch — Giaconte, Jr."

At the hospital Julie was given immediate attention. The medication put her in a slow dreamy state of mind after which a nurse got her into a private room for the night.

—⊙⌒—

Once again in the car with Sampson, Gravnick muttered, "Junior Giaconte, the little bastard." Then, "Hey, head over to Park Avenue West and Green Bay Road., where Jennifer Russo's hit and run happened."

"Didn't the beat cop check things out thoroughly?" Sampson asked.

"He could've missed something."

"Yeah, sure."

"Seriously, before we go home I need to visit some of the late night businesses around there. Someone working Saturday night might've seen something."

"Aw, come on, Chief, can't it wait until tomorrow? I'm pooped and you've already done far more than the doctor said you should."

"You know what they say — Tomorrow may never come."

"Hanging around with you, I'm gonna get dark circles under my eyes."

"You already do."

An hour and a half later, after striking out completely, Gravnick decided to try one more stop before giving in to Sampson's carping about a good night's sleep.

This time, though Gravnick had a good feeling, he gave Giaconte's mug shot to a bartender at the highland Park Country Club. "Oh, yeah," she said. "He was here Saturday night, had dinner early on in the evening with some of the members. Then he hung around the bar, putting the move on one of the member's daughters."

"You remember the name?"

"Russo."

Gravnick raised his eyebrows. "Anything else you remember?"

"Yeah. They argued, he said, "'I'll get you for this, bitch.'"

CHAPTER NINETEEN

Long before first light began seeping through the maples outside Gravnick's room at Bella Vista, he lay awake. In spite of the luxurious air foam bed, he had a bad night. He sat up, grabbed his cell, and dialed Dilly.

The phone rang several times, then, "Yah… Dilly."

"Wake up, sleepyhead."

"Who's this?"

"Me, Gravnick. I need you to get a judge to sign a warrant for Sal Giaconte, Jr."

"Christ, Gravnick. You've got to be kidding. It's not even 5 o'clock. Where am I going to find a judge at this hour?"

"I know you won't let me down. Call me soon as you get it." Gravnick clicked off and dialed another number.

"House. Here."

"Charley Horse, my old pal."

"What did I do to deserve this?" Charley House was whispering so he wouldn't wake his wife.

"My, you really are nasty…and here I am making a courtesy call to tell you that I'll be at Sal Junior's at 7, with a murder warrant."

House was suddenly wide awake. "Murder? I thought it was a hit-and-run."

"When someone runs someone down on purpose it's called murder, and I'm about to help the little bastard move into his daddy's house — the big one with the bars on the windows."

"In that case, I'm sending a SWAT team out. Could get nasty out there — especially with you around."

"I don't need a SWAT team. For god's sake, we're just picking up one man. A couple of your people will do just fine."

"Okay. But, I'm warning you, Gravnick, don't do anything until they get there."

"Charley, you know I've got the patience of a saint."

"Damn it, Ernie, I've got enough going on in this city without having you out there hot-dogging it. I'm begging you play it nice just this once."

"Absolutely, Captain, Sir."

At exactly 7 a.m., Sampson pulled the car across the street from Sal Giaconte's, Jr's. house.

"Sampson, stay put while I get the warrant from Dilly over there." Gravnick met Dilly a moment later. "Told you it was no problem."

"No problem? Right. Judge Blankington chewed me out royally. Told me never wake him again in the middle of the night or he'd have my ass on a platter."

Gravnick chuckled.

The two men's banter ended as a city patrol car parked down the street and two plain clothes officers got out and walked over to them.

"Chief Gravnick, I'm Sergeant Steve Walsh, sir."

"Good to see you here, Sergeant," Gravnick said, and turning to Dilly, introduced him.

"I don't foresee any problem but, how do you want to handle this?"

"Ring the bell. If no answer, step aside. I'll go in first in case of trouble."

Walsh said, "Detective Franks will go 'round back, and cover that for us."

As Franks disappeared around the side of the house, Walsh, Dilly, and Gravnick moved into position at the front door. Ringing the bell and then knocking loudly, Gravnick called out Giaconte's name.

"Hey, Junior, it's me, Gravnick, open up."

"Let me do this," Walsh said. Then he forcefully turned the knob. It opened.

Weapon drawn, Walsh pushed the door all the way open. Then, drawing back and to the side, he awaited a response. Not hearing or seeing anything, he moved through the door, with Gravnick and Dilly right behind him.

"Mr. Giaconte, Police."

Still hearing and seeing nothing, the three men spread out in different directions, and started a room-to-room search. In the kitchen, Dilly got a good whiff of garlic. There was a big pot of red sauce simmering on the stove. On the floor, a splash of red.

Dilly followed a trail of similar spatters. Touching his forefinger to one of them, he sensed, then smelled, the acrid odor of blood. The blood spoor went across the kitchen floor and out toward a set of open sliding glass doors leading to the patio.

Gravnick and Walsh followed Dilly to the patio where they discovered a body, or what was left of a body, still partially clad in the same gaudy smoking jacket Giaconte had worn when Gravnick and Sampson visited him. A closer look at the man's body showed the kind of pummeling meted out by the mob. A bloody baseball bat told the rest of the story.

Sergeant Walsh notified the state's attorney office, the medical examiner, and of course Charley House, whose jurisdiction it was. In Giaconte's study they found dozens of naked photographs of Jennifer Russo. The pictures had the blurred look of a hidden person clicking away secretly. Junior's chance meeting with Russo at the Highland Park Country Club had been well planned in advance. The two men completed their search and, finding nothing more in the house, Gravnick decided to pay a condolence call on Anthony Russo, father of the hit and run victim.

He found that Russo's old address on Kedzie Avenue was invalid but there was a listing for Anthony W. Russo at 146 Cody Drive in Highland Park.

"It looks like our Mr. Russo has moved up in the world. From South Kedzie in the City to Highland Park. You think he might have hit the lottery?"

"Maybe," Dilly said, chuckling.

"We can still stop there on our way back," said Gravnick.

"If you don't need me, I'll stick around here for a while and find out what I can from the M.E. before homicide takes over."

"Good idea, Jack. Sampson will drive me out there."

To make it seem like a courtesy call, Gravnick called ahead to Russo.

"This is Ernie Gravnick," he said casually, "with the Highland Park Police Department. Don't know if you remember me. I called on you in your Kedzie Avenue home a few years back while working with the Chicago police department?"

"Oh, yes. If I'm not mistaken, it's Chief Gravnick now, right?"

Ernie explained he'd been working on his daughter's case, and had some new information to update him on. "Mind if I stop by for a few moments?"

"Come right over."

Forty minutes later Sampson pulled up in front of a posh estate home that could better be described a mansion.

Russo was waiting for them. Greeting Gravnick warmly, he took them to a book-cased den with a huge mahogany desk, antique sofas, and two oversized leather chairs, where he motioned them to sit.

Russo opened with, "So, you said you had information on my Jennifer's death?"

"First let me convey my condolences and apologize for intruding on your privacy in your time of mourning," Gravnick replied. "Unfortunately, I need to ask you a few questions before I go into any particulars."

"Of course."

Gravnick asked Russo several questions he already knew the answers to. Then —"Is there anyone you know who might have wanted to harm your daughter?"

"Absolutely not. Jennifer was a wonderful girl, a great student, and well-liked by everyone that came in contact with her," Russo replied, noticeably shaken.

Gravnick said, "I'm sorry Mr. Russo, but I have one last question we need to ask. Do you have any enemies who might have done this to get back at you?"

Russo bristled. "There's no one."

Then Gravnick said, "We may know who is responsible for Jennifer's death. We're talking about a man named Salvatore Giaconte Jr."

Russo's demeanor changed from polite gentleman to a vengeful thug.

"That fucking son-of-a-bitch had dinner with me and some of my friends at the club that night. I should have known. I saw him hanging around the bar a couple of times before, but he never looked like he belonged. That night one of the guys introduced him and asked him to join us for dinner. The way he looked at Jennifer, I knew he was no good. If I get my hands on him, he's a dead man."

"It seems someone already beat you to it."

"What are you talking about — he's dead?"

"You don't get any deader," Gravnick said and added, "we're not a hundred per cent sure he's responsible."

"Course he's responsible. That little prick, I know he did it."

"How do you know that?" Gravnick asked.

Russo didn't answer right away. Shrugged. Then said, "Not sure, but thanks for coming by." He led them to the door.

In the car Gravnick sighed loudly. "Seems we're going to need more info on Russo. You know, his business, who he hangs out with, where he came from, and how he got here."

"So am I the designated researcher?" Sampson asked.

"You got it. Just keep me up to date. Hey, Julie's supposed to be home from the hospital and I promised I'd be there to have dinner with her."

As they turned into the driveway of Bella Vista. Gravnick flashed on the day before — the shock of Dylan Sullivan's bloodied body, slumped across the steering wheel — horn blaring — Julie's limp body in his arms — the single tear that fell from his eye — landing on her forehead.

Could a tear bring someone back to life? He shook his head. *What am I thinking?*

He looked up and saw Julie, standing in front of her stately home.

Ernie opened the car door, stepped out, and gallantly handed her the bouquet of roses he'd bought earlier.

"Sir Galahad, welcome to my humble abode," Julie said. "

Gravnick bowed deeply.

They kissed.

The bandage down the center of Julie's head was plainly visible.

"Cool hairdo," Gravnick remarked.

"I'm going to show it off on my next TV show. I'll have everyone wearing it."

That night the candlelit dining room and glittering crystal seemed to erase some of the horror of the previous day.

After dinner Gravnick played chess with Jonathan while Julie watched. Jonathan, for the first time showing interest in Ernie's work, questioned him about the use of photography in forensics. "Is landscape photography beginning to bore you?" Gravnick asked.

"No, but forensic photography might be kinda cool," Jonathan replied.

"Maybe one day I'll get you into the forensic lab and you can see a whole other world of photographic mastery."

"That would be great," Jonathan said. Then as Gravnick stared at Julie, realizing that even with a white head stripe she was beautiful, Jonathan completed the game of chess. "Knight takes Bishop," he said wryly.

Gravnick, said, "King to Rook. Queen to King Four." Jonathan excused himself and went to bed. Gravnick and Julie did the same.

"This could be a permanent win," she told him as she removed her clothes.

"Knight takes Queen," he said.

Chapter Twenty

Known simply by the name Roy, she sat stoically on a plain wooden chair. In front of her stood a small square table bearing no relationship to the chair, or for that matter anything else in the dimly lit, dank-smelling room.

She picked up a large insulated envelope that rested atop the table, pulled an oversized folding knife from the pocket of her dungarees, snapped it open, and expertly sliced off the top. Then deftly flicking the blade closed, she laid it gently on the table, using the other hand to simultaneously turn the envelope upside down and empty its contents on the table.

A broad smile overtook her face as she gazed at the ten stacks of bills and the sheet of paper that tumbled out. Thumbing through the bills, Roy quickly assured herself that they were all of the same denomination — each package having a thousand one hundred dollar bills. Satisfied, she picked up the letter-size sheet of paper, on which was scrawled in crayon, "For your special services." Her smile easily turned to a satisfied smirk, as she let her mind wander to the scene for which she was paid so handsomely.

She became ecstatic envisioning the smart-alecky bastard as he screamed and squirmed, her blade digging expertly, ever deeper into the well of the man's chest — then as she pulled the blade upwards, twisting it fully, so as to thrust it back down with the full weight of her on its hilt — until the little shit had gurgled. Finally, upon her weapon exiting, its special barbed end had its way, spewing blood and gore from the gaping hole it had wrought in the man's abdomen.

Still, she had to give her victim credit for having enough fight left, to stagger from the kitchen out onto the patio and even then, refused to lie down and die, until after she beat him severely around the head, shoulders and body with the baseball bat she had found standing in a corner.

Only afterwards did Roy notice that the bat had been autographed by Cubs great, Sammy Sosa. *What a waste she thought.* A lifelong Cubs fan, she would have loved to have taken it as a trophy, but ever alert, Roy knew she dare not put temptation before caution, or do anything to put herself in a position where she could be caught with anything that might tie her to her secret work. That is how she had managed to stay at the top of her profession these many years.

It is why she had always lived so frugally, in spite of amassing a large fortune that would allow her to have and do most anything she wanted. But there would be time for that later when she retired. Of course there were times she would dress up to play the part of the femme fatal, luring her unknowing prey into her web. Such play-acting was made easy for her. Under the veil of the *Plain Jane* or *John* she normally portrayed, there was an elegantly sculpted feminine body with face to match.

The last job had been a particularly enjoyable kill for Roy. She especially savored it, when a client requested that the mark, suffer a slow agonizing death. Needless to say, though she had her preferences, Roy remained the ultimate professional in her field, always ready to handle any kind of assignment. Just, like the rich bitch with her limousine and fancy home the other day. The request was to scare the living shit out of her, but leave little or no permanent scars or damage. Or the assignment she had a year or so ago that took her to Zurich Switzerland. That explosion and resulting fire was a thing of beauty. And that dim-witted cop fell right into her web, without the slightest idea of what was happening to him.

Her latest assignments, of course, were commissioned in the same way as the hundreds of others she'd handled over the many years since beginning work in her chosen career. The highly complex network of private P.O. boxes and automatic forwarding programs Roy set up across the U.S., Europe, and Asia, when first entering her profession, were all but impossible to detect, and had proven to serve her well. It not only preserved her anonymity, it protected the identity of the very select group of clients with whom she dealt. Though highly knowledgeable about today's electronic gadgets, she was aware of their faults as well, and seldom used the internet.

Actually, no one had the slightest idea who Roy was, or what she looked like. On the other hand she had never known the people that sent her the assignments, or paid her very considerable fees, always by cash in advance. Some might question that she could have just pocketed the money and walked away. But she would never consider it. That would be dishonest. Above all, she knew as a professional, her greatest asset was her integrity. Without it, she had nothing.

The clientele she dealt with were aware that Roy consistently delivered exactly what they requested, with the precision of a surgeon, no questions asked, and with no chance of an order being traced back to them. Roy was the best. True, she was outrageously expensive, but, she was worth every penny they ever paid her.

Of course Roy wasn't her real name. She had chosen it from an old western movie she had seen on television when she was a young girl. She watched a lot of television in those days. Her parents were both professionals. Her mother, a well-known attorney, was always working or traveling, and her father a famous neurosurgeon, spent most of his time either in the operating room, or lecturing at the teaching hospital.

As a result of their busy careers, Roy grew up pretty much by herself; left home alone, except for the cook Mara and houseman Paul, who paid little or no attention to her. The one exception was at bedtime, when they invariably forced her to endure their sexual perversions — threatening her life if she were ever to reveal anything.

Otherwise they left her alone to fend for herself. Watching television became her escape. She particularly liked old westerns and would fantasize about what it must have been like, growing up in the days of the Wild West. Those were exciting times when only the fittest survived. She likened herself to the best gunslinger of the times, and decided she would grow up to be the very best there was, or had ever been.

Her father had tried to interest her in becoming a surgeon and spoke to her about the respect people had for him because of the great precision required to do brain surgery. Though she had no interest in her father's career, Roy went on to earn a similar kind of respect from her clients. She knew they respected her, or they never would have paid her outrageous fees or recommended her services to others.

There was never a doubt that she would accomplish each assignment with absolute precision. The first being, the slow torturous, piece-by-piece dismemberment, of Mara and Paul, that began with cutting off Paul's unsightly testicles and penis, which were then stuffed down Mara's gagging throat. The disappearance of the cook and her houseman-husband would remain a mystery. It was the only assignment for which Roy was not remunerated in cash.

Chapter Twenty-One

The sun shone through the high cathedral windows of Julie's, now also Ernie's bedroom. It had awakened him from a dream in which he envisioned a stranger endlessly hounding him. The man was laughing out loud and mocking him. He seemed to know there was nothing Gravnick could do about it. A momentary sense of danger came over him. Then it disappeared, as his eyes were drawn back to the same stream of sun light that had awakened him. This time it was shining through the diaphanous material of Julie's negligee, as she stood in front of her mirror. "Please don't ever move from that spot," Ernie whispered.

Seeing him gawk at her, Julie tightened the negligee at her waist which made her nipples tighten. A moment later, she let her negligee fall to the floor. Gravnick's eyes roamed her body. The dark areolas, the silken patch of hair in a perfect V, her sculpted hips, every part of her was pure Julie.

～ை⌒

Forty five minutes later, Ernie was sitting in the passenger seat of his car with Sampson at the wheel. As he sipped hot coffee, his focus slipped back to the stranger in his dream.

"Have you noticed anyone hanging around or following us lately?" Gravnick asked.

"Why do you ask?"

"Not really sure. Just a weird feeling I've gotten lately. Like someone's been watching our every move. Guess I'm a little paranoid since the attack on Julie."

"That's not like you, boss," said Sampson.

"You're right, I'm not usually like this. Just the same, keep your eyes open."

"You know I've got your back."

"Speaking of having my back, we need to start thinking about your future."

"What do you mean?"

"Well, physically, I'm pretty much back to normal. But if you stay out of circulation much longer, you'll lose all of your regulars, right?"

"Are you trying to tell me I'm fired?"

"Just the opposite. I'm trying to find out if maybe you'd make a career change and come to work for us at the department."

"You want me to become a cop?"

"Well, we've been operating understaffed for some time, and with the workload picking up, we could use someone with your background. Besides, I don't feel right about letting Julie continue to foot the bill when I no longer need a baby sitter. Not only that, but I guess I've kind of gotten used to you hanging around."

After a slight pause Gravnick added, "So what do you think?"

"This is so out of the blue — I don't know. You're asking me to make a total change in my life. A cop? Really?"

"Actually, you wouldn't be just a cop," Gravnick added. "You are aware, that I've been doubling as acting Chief of Police? It looks like I'll be taking over the position permanently. As a result, I see the job I'm offering you as serving a dual purpose. First, as administrative aide to me, and second, to add extra fire power on the street. I could really use your help. You'd be getting all the perks of a cop, but bringing home a combined salary, that reflects the extra service role. Of course you'd have to go through training at the academy, but that would be a cinch, considering your experience in the military. So what do you think?"

"Well you've piqued my interest, but I'll need a couple of days to think about it."

"Take all the time you want." As Sampson pulled into the Highland Park Police parking lot, Gravnick added. "In the meantime you're still working for me, so keep your eyes peeled for anything or anyone out of the ordinary."

"Got it, Boss," Sampson said with a nod.

They stepped out of the car and Gravnick's cell phone barked. "Yeah, Jack. What's up?"

"I wanted to find out when you're coming in. I think we need to sit down and talk."

"How about right now?"

"I'd rather do it in the office if it's alright with you?" Dilly said.

"See you in three seconds."

Looking up, Dilly shook his head as Gravnick came through his doorway.

"What's going on?" Gravnick asked.

"Well, it's just that with you here part-time, I feel kind of like a fish out of water. Like I don't quite know who's in charge. Yes, I know you told me I should keep on handling things, but it's weird. I guess, I'm not really sure of how far my authority really extends."

"As far as I'm concerned, it's just like it was when you weren't sure if I was ever coming back," Gravnick said. "Being in charge means just that; being in charge. However, now that you've brought it up, I'm going to pop your bubble. I was on my way in here to thank you for doing such a bang up job in my absence. At the same time I was going to let you know that as of today, I'm back on the job. You okay with that?"

Dilly laughed, then palmed the side of his head. Extending his hand Gravnick added, "We all clear then?"

"I'm so-o-o glad you're back, boss."

Gravnick addressed the staff, informing them he'd resume full command of the Department. He also praised Jack Dilly, for having stepped up to the challenge during his absence. Formalities out of the way, Gravnick entered his office and began doing what he'd always done when the shit hit the fan.

He pulled out a legal pad from his top desk drawer and set up four columns. He headed them, *Open Cases, Status, Suspects*, and again *Status*. Returning to the left of the page, under *Open Cases* he wrote, *Winton/Wilder*, and added under *Status — Pending*.

Under *Suspects*, Gravnick listed three names: Jonathan Wilder, Julie Winton, and Unknown. Continuing to the final *Status* column, opposite each name, Gravnick entered *Jonathan — Doubtful*. After a moment of painful consideration, he hesitantly inserted *Julie Winton — Possible*. Moving to the final insertion he marked *Unknown — most probable*. In turn, he listed other open cases and their status: *The attack on Julie Winton's limo.*

Though out of his department's purview, he also listed: Zurich Bombing, Attempted hit and runs on Caron and himself, and the separate Attack to him in Zurich. He also made a notation to *look further into the life and activities of*

Anthony Russo. Finally and very deliberately, he wrote, *Continue to seek out the person or persons ultimately responsible for putting out the hit on my Grandfather that killed my father.* He looked it over and thought, *I know Giaconte, Sr. led the ambush. But who gave the actual order? I'm still not certain.*

With the above exercise completed, he called Jack Dilly and Sampson to his office, and explained his conclusions. "The department's major focus needed to be on the concept of an unknown assailant. I'm just not sure of where to begin."

"We need to determine if the unknown perp is a complete stranger, or is he, or she, for that matter, someone known to us," Dilly offered.

"If indeed it's a complete stranger, what's his motive?" Sampson asked.

"You're so right," Dilly said. "People kill for a variety of reasons — Revenge, power, money, jealousy, fear, to prove something to himself or to someone else."

Sampson cut in, "Or, just because the guy gets high by killing — a psycho." He nudged Gravnick, "You want me to continue checking on Anthony Russo?"

"Yeah, that'll keep you busy while you muse over my job offer."

"Job offer?" Dilly asked. "What job offer?"

"Sampson's thinking he might want to join our merry band of crime fighters."

Dilly shrugged. "Not a bad idea."

"Thanks for the thumbs up," Sampson said. "I guess I accept."

Gravnick reminded him even with his past experience, he'd have to go through a refresher course at the police academy. "The next training period begins soon. Meantime," Gravnick said, "take whatever time you need to settle your affairs."

A week later Sampson signed up and began his police training. Before leaving, he dropped a package on Gravnick's desk, It was an extensive report of what he'd uncovered on Anthony Russo.

Gravnick was amazed at the thoroughness of Sampson's work. He was even more surprised by Anthony Russo's business operations that reached from his junkyard business, to ownership of well-known restaurants, commercial laundries, a company that made work uniforms, collection agencies and other suspected money laundering scams for the mob.

There were links to several major labor unions as well. Gravnick shook his head and sighed as he was reading to himself. *I sure misread this guy when I first interviewed him years ago. Such a nice guy, with a young daughter, living his little life in Crumville on Kedzie Avenue. Proving his dark connection to the mob isn't going to be easy.*

It took Gravnick little time to decide his next move. To get the real dope on Russo and his activities, he'd have to revisit a life he had long left behind.

CHAPTER TWENTY-TWO

Gravnick entered the old pool hall on West Madison Street, which hadn't changed since his boyhood days. The faces differed but the characters there seemed the same. Customers at the bar still bantered over drinks and munched snacks served up, courtesy of the house. Pool sharks wielded their cue sticks, like magic wands, bidding the balls to the pockets by some secret force of will. The usual crowd stood by, watching in awe or bursting into laughter. It was all same old same old to Gravnick.

Then he heard a booming voice from the past.

"My God, is dat Ernie Gravnick?"

Gravnick turned to the hulk behind the bar. "Holy Christ, Big John. You still here? Can't be. You were a hundred when I worked here as a kid."

Big John came out from behind the battered bar that had long served up foaming brews and watered-down shots.

Gravnick at six-four, 250 pounds, was completely engulfed by Big John's smothering hug. In the next moment he was lifted from his feet — held high by giant man's hands of steel.

"Little Ernie Gravnick. Just look at ya — all growed up."

"You ugly old reprobate. Put me down, before I put you down."

Big John roared with laughter. "Ya still 'members what I taught ya? Take no shit from nobody."

Once back on the floor, Ernie remembered, as a boy doing odd jobs around the place, Big John seemed to keep an eye on him. The big man was a father figure to little Ernie, but their relationship was big bro, little bro. "Anyone gives you a problem, you be the one warns them away or gets off the first punch." To this day, Big John's simple advice had gotten Ernie into and out of a lot of trouble.

"So boy, why you slummin' down here? You ain't been 'round since you left the city for the burbs."

"Been meaning to stop by for a long time, John. You know, I do miss the old place. Lots of memories. You and Moose were mighty good to me. Saved my ass, many a time."

Hearing the clamor up front, Willie the Moose Gavanno, who had been in his office in back, emerged through the heavy oak door to the right of the bar.

"Was wonderin' what was goin' on out here," Gavanno grumbled. "Shoulda figured it was a dumb cop. Whatcha doin' here, Gravnick? Aint getting enough action in your neck of the woods?"

"Hello, Moose. Glad to see you're as ugly as ever."

Then, the two men embraced and planted double cheek kisses, Italian style.

"Been watchin' your career. What's it now? Chief Ernie?" He shook his head. "Pretty impressive."

"Yeah, well, you always were an easy touch," Gravnick said. "I gotta say this place looks the same. Probably hasn't had a coat of paint since I was last here. And the bullshit is thicker than ever. But still feels like home to me. You helped me out when my mom and I needed it most, and I'll never forget."

"Speakin' of your mom, how's Dora doing these days?"

"She's actually doing quite well, under the circumstances. Still in the home, and ornery as ever, but her mind is sharper than mine. Not bad for seventy-five and confined to a wheelchair.

Moose said, "I remember your grandfather bringing Dora here sometimes. She was maybe ten or eleven years old, and we'd leave her with Big John a few minutes, and the Don and I would go to my office to talk business. By the time we'd come out, there'd be folks crowded 'round a billiard table, cheering, as Dora whooped everybody's ass. Never seen nothing like it. But, what brings you down here? This ain't your element no more."

"Yeah, well, I've been meaning to get down here to visit just for old times, but the world keeps getting in my way," Gravnick answered.

"Don't bullshit' me. You ain't here just to look at my adoring face," Moose shot back.

"You got me, Moose. I admit, I definitely prefer looking at the ladies over you. But, yeah, you're right, I'm here for some information."

"Try me, no guarantees, understand? My office."

Seated in the old man's office that hadn't changed since Gravnick was a kid, Moose got right to the point. "Whatcha need?"

"You know anything about an Anthony Russo?"

Moose said, "Know the name. Don't know the man. Know he's supposed to be connected."

"Think you could get me something?"

"Like, what?"

"Like, who he does business with, his friends? That kind of thing."

"That's touchy. Guys like him don't 'preciate any nosin' 'round."

"That's why I'm asking you. Know you got ways of finding things."

"Well, let's just say, if I could get the info you want, what you goin' do with it? I'm askin' 'cause I don't need no unnecessary trouble. Neither do you."

"I'm sure you heard about Russo's daughter getting killed, and the thing with Giaconte Junior?"

"Yeah, been all over da news. What about 'em?"

"Well, I'm fairly certain Junior's the one responsible, but there's a few loose ends."

"Like what kind of loose ends you talkin' 'bout?"

"Come on, Moose. You know I can't reveal that kind of shit."

"Yeah, but I got to protect my reputation. I ain't jumpin' into anythin' what's gonna be a problem."

For a while, he didn't say anything. Then he reached across his desk for a cold cup of coffee. "Sometimes tastes better this way," he said with a hoarse laugh.

"Look, I just need to know if maybe it wasn't Junior. Perhaps somebody Russo did business with had a beef with him and killed his daughter."

"So, why not ask Russo?" Moose, said wiping his mouth.

Gravnick smirked. "Ah, Mr Russo, is there anyone you can think of who would want to harm you or your daughter? 'My goodness, no, there's no one. She was a wonderful girl, an outstanding student. And me….I'm a nobody…. lead a quiet life….mind my own business.' Speaking of your business, let me put it this way….do you think maybe one of those sweet guys you do business with could have something to do with your daughter's death, and was it perhaps a payoff, for the way you screwed them over?"

With a fake smile on his face Moose commented. "I guess that really wouldn't go down too good wit' Russo. Aw, right. I'll see what we can do. But no promises."

"Absolutely. I understand. Moose, I really appreciate your doing this."

"Yeah." said Moose. "Now, get out of here before I change my mind." Then standing up, signaling the end of their conversation, Moose walked out from behind the ancient desk separating them. They hugged, as before, no cheek kisses, just hard pats on the back.

On the way out, Gravnick stopped by the bar to endure another of Big John's bone breakers.

"Come back soon, Ernie me boy. Does the heart good seein' ya," John said, broken-voiced. Gravnick turned to see the big man wiping his eyes with a bar towel. Gravnick rubbed his eyes with back of his hand.

That evening Jonathan mentioned to Gravnick that he had been thinking about his offer to visit the police crime lab. "I'd really like to do that if you can make it work."

"I could probably set it up for you to see the City of Chicago's Crime lab, which is state-of-the-art."

In so doing, he thought it would give him a good chance to find out just where they were in the city's investigation of Giaconte Junior.

CHAPTER TWENTY-THREE

At 3:25 the next morning, after a pleasant night of love making, Julie lay cuddled sleep in Gravnick's arm. One minute later at 3:26, along with most of the neighboring Highland Park population, they were suddenly shaken awake by an explosion the likes of which had never happened in that high-end community of 60,000 souls.

Gravnick moved stealthily to the bedroom door. Julie was okay. She was standing on the other side of the bed. "Get down on the floor," he said. Then he opened the bedroom door and peered into the darkened hall.

Jonathan came running out of his room, nearly colliding with Gravnick. "What's happening?"

"Some kind of explosion" Gravnick said. Why are you looking at me like that?"

"Look at yourself," Jonathan said with a forced laugh.

Gravnick looked down and reddened. The *Great Protector,* gun-in-hand, stood stark naked. He began to laugh, realizing he had jumped up and ran from his room just as he had been sleeping. Julie, heard the clamor, came running out and quickly joined in the laughter.

The hilarity was short lived as they came aware of the whooshing sound coming from the other end of the hallway. Their eyes were drawn to a plume of white smoke entering the hall.

Gravnick shouted, "Get out of the house. Now."

Still carrying his gun, he ran back to the bedroom — grabbed his pants, shirt and shoes. Lastly, his cell phone. Then he turned and ran down the hall, away from the smoke. Halfway down, he pulled on his pants and thrust his feet into his shoes. Still bare-chested, he caught up with Julie and Jonathan. Momentarily, he got his shirt on. It was then he noticed his cell phone was clamped between his teeth.

At the other end of the house, where a four car garage housed Julie's limo, a sleek Ferrari sports car, and two priceless antique automobiles had stood, they saw only a big empty space and a thick knot of near flameless smoke.

Gravnick dialed 911 on his cell phone. At the same time, he scanned what had quickly become a fair sized crowd of onlookers. When he saw nothing unusual in the immediate area, he focused his attention on giving the operator information for the fire department.

He told Julie and Jonathan to stay put, then moved closer to the damaged end of the house for a closer look. To his surprise, through the dense cloud of smoke there were but a few flickering flames, a smoldering pile of ash, and molten metal — all that remained of the automobiles.

He was even more surprised when looking up to the second floor he saw a large gap in the wall, where smoke was still being sucked into the house.

Gravnick felt uneasy, as if someone was watching him. He turned again to gaze out at the crowd. He saw a handful of familiar looking neighbors that gathered near the end of the long driveway — a few had ventured halfway up, trying to get a closer view. No one seemed out of place — even the elegant, dark haired woman standing to the side of the others, looked as if she belonged.

As the fire trucks pulled up, firefighters immediately poured out like a spreading sea. They unraveled yards of hoses, then moved toward the smoking end of the building, dousing the few flaming areas that remained. As firefighters ran into the house, the commander recognized Gravnick and began to move towards him. He shouted orders for his men to turn off the air conditioner and check for hotspots inside the house.

The commander explained to Gravnick that air conditioners and heating systems cause unnecessary damage during a fire, spreading smoke and flames inside and causing sparks to flare up. Gravnick told him how they were awakened by what sounded like a huge explosion.

After a cursory look around, the commander remarked, "Without further investigation, I can't be one hundred percent certain, but everything tells me this was caused by a bomb. I'd venture that whoever planted it, was looking to cause maximum damage to the garage structure, with as little damage as possible to the house itself. It's a professional job if I ever saw one."

"What makes you so certain?" Gravnick asked.

"Because there is only minimal damage to the wall separating the house from where the garage was attached. That shows that whatever the device used, it was carefully placed and designed to explode outward, otherwise there would have been greater damage to the house itself. This guy knew exactly what he was doing."

"I have to agree with you, Commander. Seems someone is trying to send a message. But we don't know what that message is or who it's for."

Gravnick moved away from the fireman and walked back to where Julie and Jonathan were standing. Again, he scanned the crowd of bystanders. He was no longer able to see the dark-haired woman that previously caught his eye.

As he approached Julie, Gravnick saw her conversing with an elderly, hunched, little man. "Mr. Urfu here, was asking whether anyone had been in the apartment above the burned out garage. I explained that no one was living there right now."

Ernie was reminded that just mere days ago, prior to his death, Dylan Sullivan had occupied the apartment. He thought to himself; *Thank God Julie had not yet hired anyone else.*

The little man shook his head, responding in a soft, careful voice. "That is certainly fortunate. I do believe no one could have survived such an inferno. Do they have any idea what might have wreaked such havoc?"

Gravnick interrupted. "I'm sorry, sir, everything is under investigation. I'm afraid I'll have to ask you to move along and give Ms. Winton and her family some privacy."

"Oh, yes, I certainly understand," the man said, smiling politely. As he moved away Gravnick noted a gentle limp in the old man's left leg.

He turned to Julie and asked, "Who was that?"

"Mr. Urfu."

"Who in the hell is Mr. Urfu?"

"I don't know. He just showed up and began asking questions. I guess he's a neighbor. Seems harmless enough."

When Gravnick looked back, the little man had already vanished into the crowd. He scanned further, but Gravnick was unable to spot him again. Later, as Gravnick gazed towards the end of the driveway, the well-dressed, dark-haired woman reappeared. Then walked away.

The sun offered up its first glow in the eastern sky as the fire crew began its tedious task of hauling in their hoses. Before leaving, the fire chief handed Gravnick a flashlight and asked that he accompany him. Inside the house they found little damage, except for the wall where the garage had been. That was gone. The fireman flashed a beam around the other smoke-smudged walls. "If we hadn't turned off the air conditioning, this could've been worse," he commented.

Gravnick, Julie and Jonathan watched the last of the fire trucks leave. They looked at one another and shook their heads.

CHAPTER TWENTY-FOUR

As they stood outside on that brisk October morning, Julie and Jonathan in robes and slippers, Gravnick wearing the previous day's soiled clothing, they decided it was not the place to make any long term decisions.

Gravnick dialed his cell phone, caught Dilly as he left home, and recapped their situation. "As you might figure, I won't be in to work today. We need to find some clothes and a place to stay. In the meantime, Jack, I need you to get a patrolman out here to keep an eye on the place for a few hours until we can get someone to board up the windows to prevent vandals from tearing the house apart."

Dilly said, "Will do, boss. I'll get an officer over there right away. We'll also beef up the patrol that runs through the neighborhood for a couple of days. You might want to hire a guard service to keep an eye on the place until you guys move back in."

They went back inside the soot-ridden house, where Julie and Jonathan quickly donned some clothing pulled from bottom dresser drawers, and the back of closets, least affected by the smoke. They also grabbed ID's, credit cards, and pocket cash, before they walked back outside, where they both stopped to breathe the fresh air.

They hadn't eaten since the previous evening. So the first order of business was to have breakfast. They piled into Gravnick's undamaged car, then headed over to Walker Brother's on Central to fill up on hot coffee and pancakes. While waiting for their order, Julie called her assistant at Winton Cosmetics.

"Hey, Jenn, I've got a little problem. Need your help."

She explained what had happened.

Jennie Mae Wooten worked with Julie since she began the company. She knew what her boss was thinking, almost before Julie got it out of her mouth. The two of them not only had similar sounding names (Julie Winton/Jennie Wooten), they also looked enough alike that people mistook them for sisters. This worked out well when Julie needed a double to help her avoid the crowds of groupies that often followed her.

"So you need me to find a place for you to rent while you're out of the house," said Jenn.

"Yes, please call around and get me a list of two or three homes that may be available, preferably here in Highland Park."

"Will do. I'll get back to you as soon as I come up with something for you to see."

"The sooner the better, Jenn. I don't like this feeling of being homeless."

"Do you want me to make a hotel reservation for a few days?"

"I suppose we'll have to. Try the Westin, North Shore on Milwaukee Avenue. It's probably the closest decent-sized hotel. We'll need a two bedroom suite."

"Back to you soon," Jenn said. She looked up the number for the Westin North Shore.

Gravnick figured that other than the garage, the main damage to the house was smoke damage. Hopefully, most of the furnishings and clothing could be cleaned. But the smell of smoke was tough to get out. It would take time before they are able to do much about it. Before touching anything they needed to settle with the insurance company. That was going to require getting estimates for everything. In the meantime they figured they would need about a week's worth of clothes to see them through.

They spent the rest of the morning and early afternoon shopping. It took Gravnick all of forty five minutes, including being fitted for a couple of suits for work. Jonathan took even less time to grab two pair of jeans, a few polo shirts, a hoodie and a pair of sneakers. Not so with Julie. Gravnick and Jonathan found her standing close to where they had originally left her. She was holding a blouse that she examined closely. Next to her was a shopping cart, completely empty.

Gravnick asked, "What are you doing?"

"What does it look like I'm doing? I'm shopping."

"Yeah, I can see that. But, Julie honey, this is not a time to shop. It is a time to buy. At the rate you're going, we'll need to move into the store, not a hotel."

"Men," said Julie, "you'll never understand."

Three hours later, with the help and urging of both Ernie and Jonathan, Julie begrudgingly made her last great buying decision.

—◦◦◦—

That evening, after having checked into the Presidential suite of the Westin North Shore, Gravnick received a call from Jack Dilly.

"Yeah, Jack, what's happening?"

"Just got a call from Chicago homicide. Their crime lab came back with something they say you need to see."

"What is it?"

"They wouldn't tell me."

"Call them back. Tell them we've had a bad day and just checked into a hotel for a much needed night of sleep. Tell them to fax the info over and we'll take a look at it in the morning."

"I already did. They said they no could do. That it's for your eyes only."

"What kind of bullshit is that? Tell them I'll get over there sometime in the morning."

"They said right away. They said they were calling as a courtesy to you."

"I better call myself. Who did you talk to?"

"It was Captain House himself," Dilly said.

"Okay, I'll take care of it."

Gravnick picked up the phone and dialed Charley House's private number.

"What's with all the cat and mouse crap, Charley Horse?"

"Gravnick, are you on your way here?"

"No, I'm not on the way. We just checked into the Westin North Shore after a devastating night of getting burnt out of Julie's house, and a trying day of picking up clothes, and making some short term lifestyle plans."

"Yeah, I heard, and I wouldn't bother you at a time like this if there was any other way, but you need to get down here at once before all hell breaks loose."

"What are you talking about. Charley? What's so important that it can't wait until the morning?"

Charley Horse's tone changed. "We can't talk about this on the phone, and I insist you come down here now. Also, don't talk to anyone before you get here, and that includes Julie."

"What's this all about, Charley?"

"Just get down here."

"All right. I'll be there as soon as I can." Gravnick slammed the phone down.

He explained to Jonathan and Julie that he had to go out. He had police business.

"Now?" Julie asked.

"Yeah, I'm sorry. I have got to go."

With that Gravnick gave Jonathan a hug and Julie a kiss, then headed out the door. While standing in the hall, waiting for the elevator, he thought, *Why is Charley House so adamant about me not telling Julie where I'm going?*

—⊙⊙—

Night traffic was light. Gravnick took thirty five minutes to get down to his South Michigan Avenue destination. As many times as he had been to the new Chicago Police Headquarters since it's opening in 2000, Gravnick was still amazed by this technically advanced facility. The command center was a high tech hub with eight 50-inch screens. They were displayed across the front of the room, each one capable of projecting different visual images — from live newscasts to detailed mapping of targeted areas and floor plans of buildings.

Arriving outside Charley's fifth floor office, Gravnick spotted Charley standing in the hall with a blond-haired young man. House saw Gravnick, broke off his conversation with the man, and took Gravnick to his office.

"What's going on? Why am I down here? Why all the hush-hush? "

Charley House waved Gravnick over to his desk, where he had several computer readouts.

"We've gotten DNA tests back as well as a clean thumb print taken from the baseball bat found in Giaconte, Junior's home. I needed you to see these before any information is released to the public. Let me assure you, I wish I didn't have to show this to you."

Gravnick sighed. "What's going on, Charley?"

House put his arm around Ernie's shoulder. "Take a look."

Gravnick scanned the printouts. One showed a very visible thumb print.

Suddenly, he swallowed hard. The name on the bottom made his stomach a turn.

"J-U-L-I-E W-I-N-T-O-N"

"Is this a joke, Charley?"

"I wished it was. The bat was clean except for the print, and a smudge that turned out to be regurgitation of some kind. Both are a perfect match to that of Julie Winton. We did that for you at the time of her husband's murder."

Gravnick wondered, *Am I a complete fool or what?*

After a long silence, Charley said, "I'm sorry, Ernie, we've got to bring her in. The evidence puts her at the scene. With the killing of Dylan Sullivan, she had motive as well. The Grand Jury agreed and an indictment for Murder One will be issued at noon tomorrow."

Charley's mentioning of the shootings at Bella Vista brought Ernie back to reality and his mind began to calculate the timing of those events. A bell suddenly went off in his head and he shouted, "It couldn't have been Julie. There was no opportunity. She was in the hospital at the time Junior was killed."

Charley House interrupted, "It's true the records do show Ms. Winton was checked into the Highland Park Hospital at the approximate time the murder went down. We are also aware that when the floor nurse came in to check her at two a.m. and again at three a.m. on that morning, Julie Winton was not in her room. We also know that due to an emergency on the floor that night, her room was not checked again until close to 4:30 a.m., at which time the nurse indeed found her back in the room, sound asleep. But that's a period of two and one half hours! Plenty of time for Julie to have snuck out of the hospital, drive into the city, kill Giaconte, get back to the hospital and into her room again."

Gravnick shook his head. "First of all, she didn't have a car to get into the city with. Second, Julie being a restless person could well have just been taking a walk around the halls, or perhaps she went down to the cafeteria for a snack. I know she didn't eat much that night, said the hospital food was mostly inedible. Even threw up a little of it."

"We checked out both of those possibilities, but no one saw her around the hospital and it so happens that a car was reported stolen out of the hospital parking lot that night. To top it all off, hospital security strangely found it the next morning, right back where it was taken from — and as you well know, Julie is a car buff. It would have been very easy for her to pull it off."

"Of course it was Ms. Winton that reported the car stolen from the Hospital Parking lot? Come on, Charley, a child can see Julie is being set up."

"It's possible. There are always a few loose ends, but until someone proves differently, I have no choice."

Gravnick pleaded with Charley. "There must be some other answer, Charley. I just can't believe that Julie could have done any of this."

"I didn't think so either, so we questioned the nurse as to why the incident wasn't reported. Wasn't she concerned about a patient not being in her room like that in the middle of the night? Her answer to us was that she thought nothing of it at the time, because it was very normal for a patient to be taken down for various tests, such as x-rays, CAT scans and the like, during the night. But having been extremely busy on the floor, she said she hadn't noticed if an aide had come for Julie or not. She also said she didn't notice anyone bring her back."

"So that's it," Gravnick added. "She must have been taken down for a CAT scan or something. After all, she did have a head injury."

"We followed up on that too. The doctor scheduled no other tests, other than the ones they performed on her when she first arrived at the hospital. We've got means, motive and opportunity. You'll have to agree, Gravnick — we have an air-tight case."

"You're right, damn it. I can't disagree. Will you at least allow me a professional favor, of no squad cars or sirens? Let me bring her in quietly, without a press entourage and the need to disrupt all of Highland Park?"

"I agree. That's why I wanted you to be the first to know. Once this gets out it's going to be pure bedlam. But, since this is a first degree murder case, I can only give you 'til 12:00 noon, and that's pushing it."

"I understand, Charley. Thanks. It means a lot to me."

—⊙☉—

As Gravnick entered the down-elevator following his fifth floor meeting at Chicago police Headquarters, he heard a shout to hold the doors. He recognized the blond-haired man, who'd been with Charley House earlier. He wore a visitor's pass. Getting off the elevator, Gravnick had a feeling he was being watched. He glanced around and saw nothing. Just the young man slipping away. Gravnick walked toward the police parking lot, where he'd left his car.

The blond man, in reality, Roy, re-emerged, no longer a man, but a beautiful trim woman. She followed Gravnick to the parking lot, watched him get in his car and drive away. Then returning into the building, she exited out the visitor's door on the other side.

Roy walked down Michigan Avenue smiling, as she thought about how stupid the cops were. She had electronically intercepted Gravnick's call to Charley House. That enabled her to beat Gravnick downtown. With a false visitor's pass and dressed as a man, she walked right into Police Headquarters, took the elevator up to the fifth floor, and finding Captain House, walked down the hall and stopped him on the pretense of being lost. She told him she was on a group tour of the building but was now a bit lost. House told him to take the elevator down to the public information desk. He told her he was sure he would catch up with his group.

When Charley had hurried back to his office to meet with Gravnick, Roy casually followed behind. In the adjoining bathroom, with the door locked, she placed her Keltron hearing aid into her ear. The other end she pressed to the wall. She could hear the conversation clearly. Her client would be pleased as always.

That night in the suite at the Westin North Shore, Gravnick lay beside his lover and supposed murderess, Julie Winton. Somehow, she slept. He didn't. He also didn't believe it. How could such beauty be so dangerous, so duplicitous, so… beautiful? It just wasn't possible. Or was it? He tossed and turned while Julie slept like Snow White.

CHAPTER TWENTY-FIVE

In the morning, Julie sensed something was wrong. "What's going on?" she asked.

Gravnick decided to tell Julie everything straight out. He placed his hands on her shoulders, held her at arm's length, and stared directly into her eyes. "I don't quite know how to say this, and I can only couch it by saying, I have a lot of doubts. Last night when I went downtown — it turned out to be about you."

"About me? What are you talking about?"

"Chicago Homicide is issuing a bench warrant for your arrest, and they've given me until noon today to bring you in."

"Arrest for what?" Julie said, pushing him away.

"They showed me evidence that points directly to you for the murder of Salvatore Giaconte, Jr., and it looks pretty solid — including your DNA and a thumb print."

"Murder — DNA — thumb print? Are you nuts? Salvatore Giaconte, Jr, I never met the man. Don't know anything about him other than what's in the papers, or what you've told me."

Julie hesitated then looked at Gravnick with questioning eyes. Suddenly she began laughing. "Oh, I get it. It's a joke. Oh, God. I can't believe I fell for it."

"Julie, I wish I could tell you it was a joke, but I'm dead serious — and from the evidence I saw, it's going to be hard to prove otherwise. You need to call your attorney and take care of whatever else you need to do."

"Why? This is nonsense. I didn't do anything."

"I know, and I have to admit there are a lot of unanswered questions, but the reality is that they have a strong case against you. In the meantime, please get yourself together. It's now eight fifteen, and I have to have you at police head-quarters downtown by noon. Also, as the charge is be first degree murder, don't expect to be coming home again anytime soon."

Pulling away from him, Julie flushed with anger. "Look, I'm not going anywhere with you or anyone else. This is absolutely ridiculous. First of all, I hav-en't the slightest clue as to where this Giaconte guy lived, what he looked like, or anything else. And tell me just when was I supposed to have done this *dastardly* deed?"

"The night you were in the hospital," Gravnick answered.

"The night I was in the hospital? Yeah sure. How was I supposed to have done that? Was it an out-of-body experience? While I was in the hospital, my vengeful spirit ran all around town committing crimes. Tell me how I managed to be in two places at the same time?"

"According to hospital records, you were missing from your room for up to three and a half hours that night, and no one in the hospital remembered seeing you from one a.m. to four thirty a.m."

Julie shook her head. " I never left my room. As a matter of fact, it seemed like everyone but the janitor stopped in that night. Every time I fell asleep, some-one came in and woke me. The regular floor nurse popped in every hour on the hour, and others came in between to check my temperature, draw blood, get a urine sample, or whatever else the doctor ordered. Even the plumber came in to fix the shower in the bathroom, which he said someone complained about."

"The plumber? What time was that?"

"Oh, I don't know." She stopped a moment, as if remembering something else, then went on. "Actually, I might have been out of my room for a period that night. I…I'm not sure, though…"

"What do you mean, you're not sure?"

"I remember a heavy-set aide coming in with a gurney. Said he had to take me down stairs for an MRI. I told him they already had an MRI, but he explained that something wasn't right with it and that the doctor had ordered another one."

"An MRI? What time was that?"

"It was right after the night nurse came in on her regular rounds. I'd dozed off and I remember looking at the clock and thinking that it's impossible to sleep in a hospital — everyone coming or going, day and night. It was about ten after one in the morning when he came in…but, there's a weird piece of missing time…I don't remember him or anyone else taking me downstairs — or actually getting the MRI — or anyone bringing me back to the room. As a matter of fact, I don't remember anything else about the rest of that night, until the nurse came in around six o'clock to take a blood sample."

"The aide that came in to take you down — do you recall what he looked like?"

"He was hard to forget. Hispanic, fat, probably 300 pounds, five foot eight or nine, a scratchy high-pitched voice, heavy accent. Why?"

Gravnick realized her answers didn't jive with the hospital records, but nevertheless playing it close to the belt, he answered, "Oh nothing, I just want to check out a few things."

"Check out all you want. I can't believe you fell for all this crap. You of all people."

Gravnick took a deep breath. Even in her anger, she was lovely to look at. "Look, the city cops have plenty of evidence to bring you in, and it's completely out of my hands. I must insist you get dressed and do what you have to do. Otherwise, I'm going to have to arrest you myself, and take you in cuffs, in a squad car with sirens blazing. I'm sure the press will have an absolute field day with that. I can see it now. *Highland Park Homicide Chief arrests girlfriend — turns her over to Chicago cops. TV personality and business mogul Julie Winton charged with murder of Chicago mobster, Salvatore Giaconte Jr.'*

"You wouldn't?"

"Oh, yes I would. I don't want to, but if you give me no other choice…" Gravnick's voice trailed off. He rubbed his eyes. He'd never been so tired, so frayed — and, he had to admit — so blindly in love.

Julie said, "I object, strongly, but I need to get a hold of Jenn Wooten. She'll have to take over my schedule as best as possible. Oh, shit, this couldn't have come at a worse time. I'm scheduled to leave for the Far East next week, and then on to Paris to put on a special Fashion Week exhibit." She hesitated, her mind leaping from one fragmented thought to another.

"Well, Jenn will just have to manage it on her own. I guess that's what I've been grooming her for anyway; to someday take over for me." After another short moment, her mind still racing, she turned and stared directly at Gravnick. "And you. You will take custody of Jonathan until this thing is over or, whatever else may come of it."

"What are you talking about? I'm in no position to take custody of Jonathan. Isn't there anyone else? An aunt or uncle — don't you have a cousin?"

"There is no one else I trust," Julie stated unequivocally. Besides, he loves being with you and I know you love him."

"But I'm on call all hours of the day and night. I couldn't always be here for him." Ernie continued to find excuses.

"With my career, I haven't always been around either. Jonathan, as you know, is very self-sufficient and used to being home alone with Dylan Sullivan or another one of the household staff," Julie explained.

Still Gravnick objected. "Well, Dylan Sullivan is no longer around to keep an eye on him, and at this juncture, we no longer have a house or any household help either."

In a strangely reasonable voice, Julie replied, "You'll find suitable temporary housing in the next few days and I'll have Jenn hire a nanny to keep an eye on Jonathan *and* you. She'll also see that you get a proper allowance to run the house and care for Jonathan's needs. Now, if you have no more silly excuses I have a lot details to go over with Jenn."

Gravnick said, in the same calm manner, "Please get done already. Oh, and while you're talking to Jenn, tell her to have your attorney meet us downtown at Chicago Police Headquarters." Gravnick shook his head in complete surrender. He'd manage with Jonathan.

CHAPTER TWENTY-SIX

At eleven thirty-four that morning, Gravnick and Julie Winton were hand-in-hand and face-to-face, in an up elevator at Chicago's Police Headquarters. As he quietly offered words of encouragement, Julie touched a finger to his lips.

"I know you'll find the person or persons behind all this — I'll be just fine."

"I'll do what I can." Gravnick said. "But this is going to be a rough one and I can't give you any guarantees. Whatever goes down just remember, I love you very much. Most of all, I won't give up on you."

The elevator came to a stop. The doors opened. Facing them were two uniformed officers and Captain House, who thanked her for surrendering. Before either of them could say a word Charley read Julie her rights. One of the officers motioned her to put her hands behind her back. He snapped on a pair of cuffs, and together with the other uniform, whisked her away down the hall to a second bank of elevators that took them directly down to booking.

Gravnick watched as Julie stepped into the elevator. The doors closed.

"Charley, was all that necessary?"

"Yeah it was. These halls tend to have big eyes and ears. The longer she hung around, the more chance there is of word getting out that we've got her in custody. You know the press will be all over this soon enough. For both your sakes, I want her to at least have a chance to meet with her attorney first. He's waiting downstairs right now."

"I guess you're right. The poor kid is scared to death."

"And scared she should be." Charley added. "Though there are a few open questions, the evidence is enough for an indictment and possible conviction.

"Open questions, I would explain it more like gaping holes." With that Gravnick pushed the down button. The elevator doors opened.

"Tell me, what you're referring to," House asked.

"No."

The elevator doors closed leaving House thinking, *what a schmuck I am. I tried to be a nice guy, and if I know Gravnick, I'll be the one who ends up with egg on my face.*

"Damn you, Gravnick," he exclaimed.

Gravnick headed West on I-94 on his way back to Highland Park. He finished one phone call, and immediately after, dialed Jack Dilly.

"Captain Dilly, here."

"Yeah, Jack, I need you to get over to the hospital on Highland Park, West, right now. Pick up all their video surveillance tapes for the day Julie was in the hospital, from the time she was admitted until she was discharged."

"If they won't give them to me, do you want me to get a subpoena?"

"You won't need a subpoena. I already spoke to the administrator and she'll have them waiting for you."

"I just love when you work you're magic with the women, Gravnick. It makes my life so much easier," Jack mused.

"Yeah, right. Just get over there. Have them ready for me by the time I get back."

"I hear you, Boss."

CHAPTER TWENTY-SEVEN

Paul Diamond was a short, squat, man with a kind face, smiling eyes, an a soft rural accent. The sort of person everyone is drawn to. One of those people who exudes trust and integrity. In addition he was known to be one of the best defense attorneys in Chicago.

As the elevator door opened revealing Julie and the two officers who accompanied her, Diamond was there to greet them. He offered an enthusiastic smile and a comforting hug to his client. He followed with a knowing nod to the two police officers.

"Joe, Phil. You take good care of my lady here. See that she gets whatever she wants."

"Sure, Mr. Diamond. It isn't often we have an international celebrity visiting us," the lead officer responded.

"Julie, the boys here have to take you down to booking. I'll see you as soon as they finish up. Okay?"

"Thank you, Paul, I appreciate your getting here so quickly."

"See you in a bit."

Diamond had read the indictment as soon as he arrived, and was already thinking how he was going to defend Julie. Though he hadn't had time to examine the actual physical evidence, he could see that much of it was circumstantial. *The beautiful thing about our judicial system is that, the prosecution bears the full burden of proof beyond a reasonable doubt.* The defense doesn't have to prove a thing. He needed only to plant a seed of doubt in the head of one juror. To do this, not only required a fine knowledge of the law, but a great defense attorney needed to be a plotter, a plodder, a psychologist, have the presence of an Oscar winning performer, and last, the creative imagination of a novelist.

Paul Diamond had all the moving parts assembled like the finest Swiss watch. The result was, in almost twenty years of practicing law he had never let a client down. He had never lost a case. His phone rang. Might this call change his batting average?

"Hello, this is Paul Diamond."

The voice Diamond heard was like no other he had heard before. Somewhat high-pitched, yet male sounding, a little distorted, but most of all, creepy.

"Mr. Diamond, I am so glad you answer your own phone. It makes everything so much easier. Don't you think?"

"I beg your pardon. Who is this?"

"I'm no one you need to know, or really want to know."

Annoyed and figuring it a prank, Paul snapped, "Okay, whoever you are, I don't have time to play games. Tell me who this is or I am hanging up."

"Sir, if you really must know, I'm your worst nightmare. Not only won't you hang up, Mr. Diamond, but you're going to do exactly as I tell you, or something very bad could happen to that beautiful wife and two daughters of yours."

Paul exploded. "Now listen here. If you go anywhere near my family I'll…"

The voice over the phone sounded even more sinister, "You are not listening to me Mr. Diamond. All you need to do is lose the first case of your outstanding career, in your upcoming defense of Julie Winton."

Surprised, Paul questioned, "I just got the case. How could you even know? Who in the hell are you anyway?"

"As I told you no one you want to know. So, I suggest you merely heed our warning, and we will make sure it stays that way. Ignore this warning and your wife and children will die excruciating deaths."

"You son-of-a-bitch," Diamond said.

"No, Mr. Diamond — I talk, you listen." The voice, turned deadly. "You are not taking my warning seriously. Under the circumstances, I suggest you call your wife's cell phone number. I believe she'll convince you of the significance of this conversation. I'm hanging up so you can call now."

As the call clicked off, Paul Diamond found his hands shaking. He called his wife. The person that answered had the same eerie voice that just hung up on him.

"Hello, again, Mr. Diamond. Or, may I call you Paul?" The voice asked.

Paul Diamond ignored the caller's question.

"Where is my wife, and how did you get her cell phone?"

"You still don't seem to be hearing me. I speak and you listen. Can you do that Paul?"

For the first time in his adult life, Diamond felt frightened. He began to lose control. He said quietly, "Are my wife and family all right?"

"That's much better, Paul. I take it that you do approve of my calling you Paul?"

"Yes."

"That's nice, real nice. Now here's your wife."

"Paul, is that you? What is going on? Who are these people? Please, Paul, whatever they want, give it to them."

"Irena, are you all right? Are the girls all right?"

"Yes, we're all okay. Just get us out of here." Irena began to sob. In the background he heard his girls crying. His heart stopped.

Before Diamond could speak again, the strange voice was back on the phone.

"That's enough for now, Paul. I want you to understand that you have no choice but to do what we ask of you. You do understand, don't you, Paul?"

Paul Diamond answered, "Yes, yes, but a murder trial will take months, possibly longer. What will happen to my family? Others will find out they are missing. Questions will be asked. How will I answer them? If I don't properly represent my client, the authorities will know something's wrong."

"First of all, you will see that the case never goes to trial. You are to get your client to plead guilty to all charges. Second, your family will be back in your home with you this evening. No one will know anything. Except for them, and of course you, Paul. But, be aware that we can take them from you any time. As the smart man I know you are, you no doubt have already figured this out. Our eyes are everywhere. Even if you were to try hiding them or surround them with 24 hour security, you need to understand, all of it would be totally useless." The voice was suddenly joyful, "So, I take it we have a mutual understanding, don't we, Paul?"

The best Diamond could do was say, "Yes."

"Wunderbar." was the last thing he heard before the phone went dead.

—◦◦—

The booking process completed, Julie sat anxiously in a cell awaiting her attorney. *Thank God for Paul Diamond,* she thought. *He'll be down in a few minutes and he'll know just what to do. He'll have me out of here before I know it and this nightmare will be over.*

Unbeknownst to her, Diamond was far too distraught to face his client at the moment. He needed time to rethink his position. He left the building.

By the time Diamond returned the following morning Julie, not knowing what happened to him and unable to make any more phone calls had all but torn the jail down. Even Gravnick had seemingly abandoned her, believing that she would be meeting with her attorney after being booked. As a guard escorted Julie into the visitor's area she was seething.

Upon seeing Paul, Julie blurted out, "You son-of-a-bitch, what in hell happened to you? You told me we'd meet after I was booked and instead you left me sitting here in a cell all night long with no idea of where you were or what was happening to me. What's going on, Paul?"

"You want to know what's going on," Diamond said. "Okay, but this isn't easy and you're not going to like what I have to tell you."

"I'm not a child. Whatever it is, get it out."

"Last night I took the time to look deep into the evidence. The case they've got is totally stacked against you. I'm sorry Julie, but the truth is they have you dead to rights. The best advice I can give you, not just as your attorney, but as a friend, is to declare yourself guilty and throw yourself on the mercy of the court."

"Are you completely crazy?" Julie shouted. "Declare myself guilty — guilty of what? I didn't do anything. No, I will not declare myself guilty — and further, I want out of here — and I want out now. Start doing what I'm paying you for."

"You're not going anywhere, except to make an initial appearance in court before noon today. Furthermore since you are under a grand jury indictment, you will be facing arraignment at the same time, so we need to get you prepped right now."

"Prepped for what? The gallows?"

Diamond started to answer, but was cut off by Julie.

"Look, Paul, if there is no reasonable way to defend me — come up with an unreasonable way. I don't care how you do it, just do your job, or I'll get another lawyer. Where the hell is Gravnick? He said he'd keep me posted of any new findings."

Diamond shrugged. "I'm sure Chief Gravnick would have been in touch if there were any new findings."

"Don't you get it? I'm being set up. Who or why it's happening, I've absolutely no clue. But I'm sure Gravnick will get to the truth. In the meantime there's is no way I'm going to plead guilty for something I didn't do."

Diamond had to stall for time. "If you insist on being stubborn, I'll try to figure out some alternative defense. God knows, right now, I haven't a clue where to go with this."

"You're the best there is, Paul, so don't screw up." Julie's appearance in court went just about as Paul Diamond had explained. The clerk read the charge of "Murder in the first degree." The judge asked Julie how she pleaded, and she responded "Not Guilty Your Honor," followed by the judge ordering her held without bail in Cook County Jail until a court date could be set. Though already knowing the judge would turn him down, Diamond pleaded leniency, asking that she be allowed to serve bail under house arrest with electronic surveillance.

The judge answered that he should know better than to waste the court's time. "You know the law prescribes no bail in first degree murder cases. Turning to Julie he says, "And you missy, just because you have money and big tits, doesn't put you above the law."

Hearing this, Julie lost her temper, yelled at the judge where upon he charged her with contempt and fined her $10,000. Julie refused to quiet down and threatening legal action against the judge, to have him "removed from the bench for sexual harassment, and extreme prejudice against women"— as well as a slew of other charges — leading the judge to up the contempt charge to $100,000.

Later seated in her cell Julie began to wonder, *what in hell is going on here? This whole thing seems to be turning into a conspiracy against me. Who would go to such lengths to set this up — even a judge who is hell-bent on taking his obvious prejudice against women, out on me — and my own attorney appears to be fighting me by stalling and disagreeing with every suggestion I make. Oh Gravnick. Where are you? I really need you. You son-of a bitch, I need you — now."*

As if she waved a magic wand a guard entered the cell block shouting, "Winton, get it together. You've got a visitor."

Julie spotted Gravnick's face as she entered the visitor's area and immediately walked to the glass area separating the prisoners from their visitors.

"Hello," he said softly into the speaker phone as she picked up on her end.

"Hello, my ass. Where in hell have you been? The world has fallen apart and you're nowhere to be found."

"That's a heck of a way to greet a guest."

Julie spent the next several minutes spewing the details of her incarceration and court experience.

"Dilly's is hunting down the video tapes from your hospital stay. Hopefully we'll find something to counter the evidence the police have come up with."

"As far as your first question, where I've been…Jenn came up with a few houses for us to look at and we found a place in our same school district, which will work out great for Jonathan. It's just a six or seven month lease, which should be plenty of time for the contractor to get Bella Vista back up to move-in condition."

"Well, at least something seems to be going right. But I'd appreciate your speaking with Paul Diamond for me. Something's just not right with him. It's like he doesn't want to defend me."

"Who knows? But I'll speak to him."

"Just get me out of here, will you Gravnick?"

After leaving, he called Paul Diamond. When the attorney realized that Gravnick wasn't going to go away without a full explanation, he decided to play nice and invited him to breakfast.

"Could we do an early breakfast tomorrow? Say, 7 a.m.?"

"That works." Gravnick answered.

"Great, I'll arrange eggs benedict in my office. Okay?"

"Yeah, see you in the morning."

CHAPTER TWENTY-EIGHT

On his way back to the Highland Park police station Ernie called Dilly to make sure the video recordings he was to pick up from the hospital were set up and ready for him to view upon his arrival.

"Everything's all set Chief, We've also have a surprise waiting here for you as well."

"You know I don't like surprises."

"I think you'll be pleased with this one," Dilly said.

―⊙⊙―

A little later, Gravnick entered Dilly's office. Sampson was there, smiling.

"I've finished my training and I'm ready to go to work."

"Well, nobody notified me. I was to be at your graduation. Seems everyone's forgotten I'm still in charge around here."

"I'm sorry, boss. I assumed the academy told you."

"Well, you thought wrong. I never heard a word. But if you're going to work here, never assume anything."

"Gotcha, boss. Won't happen again."

"Dilly has some videos for us to look at, but come with me first.

Gravnick walked to his office. Sampson followed. He opened his desk drawer and pulled out a shield.

"If you're going to be a cop you'll need to have a badge."

Sampson stared in disbelief. "This is a detective's shield," he said.

"Hang on to it," Gravnick told him.

"You're kidding" Sampson sputtered.

"Let's get to work, Detective."

"Right with you, sir."

Moments later, they sat with Dilly in front of a large screen.

"These videos cover the time period of Julie's stay in the hospital from when she was brought into the emergency room until she was signed out." Dilly explained.

"What are we looking for?" Sampson asked.

"Anything that's out of the ordinary," Gravnick said.

The three men stared intently at the screen for some time, as the images unfolded.

Gravnick caught himself feeling sleepy from the visual barrage of irrelevant movement. "Stop the tape. This isn't working. We need to break this up one image at a time."

"Yeah, you're right," Dilly agreed.

"Maybe we should do this two at a time, with frequent breaks," Sampson suggested.

Gravnick left Sampson and Dilly to their slow perusal. He needed some sleep before his early morning breakfast with Paul Diamond.

As he drove back to the Windom North Shore, Gravnick wondered how a city with so many people — a virtual honeycomb — could maintain itself with all the murders, madness, court orders, accusations, explosions, implosions and delirium that whirled around like a human cyclone. "That's my life," Gravnick said aloud. "Like it or not."

Alone in his study, Paul Diamond sat in an overstuffed chair he believed was the best purchase he'd ever made. Deep in thought, he pondered his next actions; whether to betray everything he'd always believed in — had taken an oath to uphold or — whether to play it safe, by following the orders given him by the voice on the phone...or...

He told himself he should stay true to his principles by using the morning meeting, to tell all to Gravnick, and seek police protection for himself and his family. This is what he really wanted to do. Still he knew that should anything go wrong and something were to happen to his family he could never forgive himself.

His mind went doggedly back and forth, until finally, after many deep breaths, he made the decision, he knew he must make. He would bite the bullet and let Gravnick take it from there. With the one decision out of the way, he could at last relax. With his mind finally at ease, he turned to the 10 o'clock news on WGN for the latest update. After less than a half an hour of the usual inner-city, night-time tribulations, he flipped off the tube and retired for what he hoped would be a good night's sleep.

It seemed only minutes later when the phone rang. A soft spoken voice said, "I hope I didn't wake you, Paul. But, you know what? I've been sitting here thinking that we haven't talked since yesterday. And do you know what else? It suddenly dawned on me that though I know you are a man of your word and that you absolutely want to do the right thing, a lack of proper communication can easily allow doubt to subdue one's good intentions. You know what I mean, don't you, Paul?"

Paul knew. Even in his sleeping-pill-induced stupor, he knew. Though he had fooled himself into believing he could make it go away, he knew that some people never go away. Once they get their claws into you they never let go. Hearing it at this ungodly hour, Paul shook with fear.

"You still there Paul?"

Diamond barely managed to whisper, "Yes."

"And you understand what I mean don't you, Paul?"

"Yes."

"Oh, that's very good. Now do try to get some sleep, won't you, Paul?" Roy set the phone back in its cradle and began to laugh out loud.

—◦◉◦—

By 6:30 that morning, Diamond sat at a round table clothed in white Damask, set with blue and white Wedgewood, complimented by sterling flatware, and French linen napkins, all specifically ordered to his office for the occasion. There was even a person to attend to every whim of his guest, whom he intended to show, that contrary to the impression previously offered, he now wished to welcome him with open arms.

Though he thought he would simply be asking Gravnick for help, circumstances had again changed because of the unsettling night phone call. He must use every wit of persuasion to convince Gravnick that he would continue to defend Julie Winton as no other attorney possibly could. Though he intended not to win the case, he not only needed to make his defense look good, he must, somehow make Gravnick believe that Julie was guilty.

Gravnick opened the door to Diamond's office and was immediately met by a well-mannered young man, who escorted him to the table. Paul stood up to greet him.

"Good morning." Diamond said cheerfully offering Gravnick an extended hand.

"I do hope you're hungry. I am told that Fredrick here is noted for his Eggs Benedict."

The young man smiled politely and asked Gravnick, "Would you prefer your Eggs Benedict, regular, Florentine or…"

"As they were meant to be. The good old fashioned way."

"Yes sir, I know what you mean, sir."

As the man eased back on his way to the portable kitchen, set at the other end of the room Gravnick suffered a fleeting shiver, immediately forgotten, as Diamond interrupted, and the two men were quickly drawn into deep conversation.

Paul jumped right in with a haymaker, "Gravnick, I'm going to be totally up front. Julie Winton, meaning we, are in big time trouble."

"What do you know that I don't know, Paul?"

A little thrown by Ernie's easy comeback, Diamond responded, "What I mean is that the State has a cache of extremely explosive evidence on their side and they are out to prove that they don't play favorites when it comes to the rich and powerful. They intend to set a precedent on this one."

"Bullshit," Gravnick said. "What they've got is ninety-nine percent circumstantial."

"True, but there's an overwhelming amount of it. Along with her DNA, fingerprint being found at the scene, her disappearance from the hospital during the time of the murder — These make it impossible for a jury to turn a blind eye."

"I take it you mean her apparent disappearance?" Gravnick said.

"Well, yes, the fact is no one could verify where she was at the time."

"That's what they say, but we're looking further into that one. I think we'll find it's not what it seems. It's also possible the real killer somehow lifted her print from something else to purposely set her up. Regardless, tell me what are you going to do about it? I want to hear how you're defending Julie."

"Look Ernie you know I've never lost a case and this bothers me no end. As someone who has long prided himself on success, I can't see anything but failure here."

"Then get it out of your mind."

"I wish it were that simple. The best chance we have of preventing Julie from getting life or possibly a death sentence, would be for her to plead guilty and throw herself on the mercy of the court."

"How about you stop and tell me what's really going on, Paul."

"Look Gravnick, nothing is going on. I'm pointing out the legal point of view from where we sit."

Gravnick drank his champagne in one clean gulp. "It may be where *you* sit, Sir," he said, "but it is not from where I'm sitting. And, it isn't anywhere near what I expect for Julie Winton. So either you start being real about a defense, or I will be recommending another attorney."

The young waiter returned with their platters, which he carefully set on a serving stand and efficiently began to serve.

"Thank you, Fredrick," Paul said with a nod.

Fredrick gave a slight bow, pivoted gracefully and walked away.

"As I see it we need to build a parallel case based on the suppositions you've mentioned, along with the other circumstantial evidence the state will be using. More importantly while I do my research, I need some further evidence to shore up her case."

"Is there anything special you want from me?" Gravnick asked.

"Well, you brought up the time-line when Julie was missing from the hospital."

"Allegedly missing." Gravnick corrected.

"Ah, yes, allegedly missing. Is there something else you want to tell me?"

"Only that we are going over the hospital surveillance videos for the entire time Julie was there and if there is anything at all in them we are going to find it."

"Excellent, anything that disproves the timeline can help — and that goes double for the finger print."

All the while, Roy, doing a flawless Fredrick — the young man from the catering company — had imperceptibly been busying himself with kitchen clean up. He'd also been tuned to the conversation and was recording it with a hidden audio device.

He was also sure her role as fat man pushing the gurney down the hospital hall was a complete success. Nevertheless, she'd leave nothing to chance.

After settling the caterer's bill, Paul Diamond sat on the leather executive chair behind his grand desk. He too, was certain of something — that his meeting with Gravnick was a total bust. He was devastated. He was thinking about how he might change Gravnick's mind when his phone rang.

"Shame on you, Paul." the voice said mockingly. "You certainly screwed up, groveling at Gravnick's feet like that."

"How do you know?"

"I told you, we have eyes and ears everywhere."

Diamond's heart stopped, then leaped and galloped.

"I certainly hope we don't have to revisit that beautiful family of yours, Paul. It would be a real shame to upset them again. Your little Ilene, getting ready to go away to school and all. It'd be a pity to shake her confidence in you."

"I assure you I can handle Gravnick."

"And just how are you going to do that?"

"I have a plan."

"I'm all ears, Paul."

"Actually I'm still working it out but, I'm feeling confident that I can win him over."

"I see. Like you did this morning."

"It's going to work. I promise."

"Your promises mean nothing. I should save myself some time and …"

"Don't do anything. Please. Gravnick will co-operate."

"All right, Paul. I'm going to be lenient just this once. You've got five days, 120 hours to handle Gravnick and get Julie Winton to take a guilty plea."

CHAPTER TWENTY-NINE

After Gravnick left Diamond's office, he had an unsettling feeling that the waiter was someone he'd seen before. His animal instinct told him that the man's fey movements as he prepared and served the breakfast were a little unusual…rather off-putting he thought…but why? Then he flashed on the disappearing woman at the Belle Vista fire. She seemed to fade away just like the waiter. The mind and its monkey tricks, he thought.

Sampson and Jack Dilly were secluded in Dilly's office reviewing more of the hospital tapes when Gravnick walked in.

"Hey, boss." Dilly said.

"Found anything?" Gravnick questioned.

Sampson said, "maybe it's nothing. But I came across a clip of this the short, fat orderly, the one Julie described to you."

"I'd like to see that. Bring it back up." Gravnick ordered.

"It'll take a minute. I marked it, figuring you'd want to see it. The guy came out wheeling a gurney with someone on it. Then he took it out to where the ambulances come and go. But, there was no ambulance around — just a four-door, dark gray Buick sedan, parked under the *Ambulances Only* sign."

Sampson found the clip and showed Gravnick. Here was the obese orderly, plain to see. He seemed to struggle with the patient. But once he got him into the Buick, he slammed the door shut. Then proceeded to take the empty gurney to a dark area under the stairwell as if to conceal it from view. Afterwards, he turned and ran back to the car, jumped in, and drove off with the patient.

"Makes no sense," Sampson said. Dilly added, "Looks like a bad TV show."

"Show it again, Sampson," He rewound the tape and all three watched very closely.

"Wait. Stop it there." Gravnick said. Sampson freeze-framed it.

"What's up, Boss?"

It's a feeling. Like a shiver. I've had it before. Happened after the fire, and in the city at police headquarters. Had the same feeling this morning while meeting with Julie's lawyer."

"What's it like? Sampson asked.

"Like I said, a kind of shiver — like when you sense danger and you don't know why."

"Are you talking about the hospital attendant?" Dilly said.

"Yes, and more," Gravnick said.

"More what?" Dilly asked.

"Looks like he's more than a man…"

"Right," Sampson said, "he sure is a fatso."

"Not when he moves, like a ballet dancer. Check the video again." Gravnick said. "See if you can see the license plate. The car in the hospital taken from parking lot was a Buick, like that one. If we can get the license number…"

CHAPTER THIRTY

Dora Gravnick awakened with a rare smile on her face. It was Sunday. She was expecting her son's usual visit to the Deerfield Nursing Home, except that he missed the past two weeks due to a "big case" and she was more excited now than usual. Dora understood that work must come first. But today she hoped he'd show up with that lovely Julie Winton. Aside from seeing her bachelor son in a serious relationship with a woman, she just plain enjoyed having Julie around. "That girl makes me feel good." There were few things anymore that brought a smile to Dora's face.

As she lay there awaiting the nurse to get her ready for the day, Dora was aware of someone standing in the doorway. "Is that you Melony?"

She called again, "Hello." Then, "Whoever you are, you're scaring me." Since the stroke she'd lost all ability to move any part of her body. But somehow she managed to scrunch her head just far enough to see a short fat orderly, melt away into the hall.

A moment later, Melony came running into her room.

"Dora what's wrong? Oh my. Who moved you around like that?"

"Did you see him?" Dora said, still scared.

"Who?"

"The man in the doorway. A short, fat guy. An orderly."

"I didn't see anyone coming towards the nurse's station," she said as she moved back out the door and peered down the hall.

"There's no one out here now. You say you saw someone standing by your door?"

"Yes, he stood there purposely taunting me. Even after I told him he was scaring me."

"You said he was short and fat?"

"— and ugly." Dora added.

"No one like that works here." Melony said. "I'd better notify security right now."

By the time she returned Melony noticed that Dora had already calmed down.

"I told security to stop anyone answering the description you gave and to call the police immediately. In the meantime I should notify Chief Gravnick?"

"Don't bother. He'll be coming by shortly anyway." Dora answered.

"All right. But are you going to be okay by yourself 'til I get back?"

"Of course. Go. Do what you do."

"Okay, but I'll come back shortly and get you bathed and dressed."

"Yah. Yah. Go already." Dora chided.

A few minutes later a woman's head peered discreetly from the shadow of the janitor's closet at the end of the hall. Assured the area was clear she moved out smoothly, revealing a carefully quaffed hair-do and fine facial features. Without looking around she glided to the nearby lobby area where she smiled and waved goodbye to the security guard at the front desk. Roy exited the main entrance, carrying a small duffle containing orderly's gear, and continued smiling as she spotted the parking lot guard, who eyed her up and down. A couple of minutes later, as she drove through the front gate, she gave the guard the finger. Her smile turned to a full blown laugh. *"That'll give Gravnick something to be concerned about. Maybe he'll spend less time snooping around about his girlfriend."*

Prior to his usual Sunday visit with Dora at the nursing home, Gravnick visited with Julie to bring her up to date on his meeting with Diamond. "There's some hope," he said.

"I still think Paul's jerking me around," Julie said.

"What exactly does he do or not do that bothers you?"

"When I call, I'm told he's not available or he's out of the office. He'll let me sit for a day or two before getting back to me and when he finally does call he gives me some half-ass reason for making me wait. Then he assures me that he's got everything under control."

"I'll get to the bottom of this, I promise."

"I'm sure you will. But will it be in time to save me? I don't want to rot away in this hole or worse, hang by the neck until dead."

"They don't do that anymore." He was glad to see she still had her spirit.

CHAPTER THIRTY-ONE

A uniformed patrolman entered the Highland Park Police Station, sauntered past the duty officer with a casual salute. "Hey, Ed. How's the world?"

Without looking up from the TV the officer answered, "Been a quiet Sunday night so far."

The patrolman said, "Let's hope it stays that way."

"Amen," the duty officer murmured.

The patrolman, knowing exactly where to go, walked back around the corner to Jack Dilly's office, and using a lock-pick opened the door to the darkened room. A few weeks ago, Roy posing as a substitute teacher, (having removed the real teacher) had brought a class of children on a tour of the police station. She knew what to look for — the small safe in the corner.

A few minutes later, the patrol officer nonchalantly walked back past the duty desk and casually said, "Catch you tomorrow, Ed."

Glancing briefly away from the TV, the duty man grunted, "Uh-huh."

Roy exited the police station and headed home. The hospital tapes, meanwhile lay disintegrated in Dilly's safe. "Battery acid works every time," Roy told herself with professional pride.

—⟳⟲—

Gravnick arrived at Dora's nursing home and moved past the nurse's station.

"Oh, Chief Gravnick. May I speak to you for a moment?"

"Certainly, Melony," he said. "Everything okay?"

"I don't really know," Melony began. "We had an incident with Dora this morning."

"What kind of incident? Is she okay?"

"Yes everything's okay now, but, earlier she called out suddenly. By the time I got to her she was turned in her bed and staring at the door. She was saying, 'Did you see him?'

"I asked who. She said, 'The man in the doorway? He was right there — you couldn't miss him. He was short, fat and — ugly. Dressed like an aide.' She told me that he taunted her. 'Just stood there — not saying a word.'"

"Then what?" Gravnick questioned.

"I checked the hall but no one was around. Just the same she was so shaken up, and the way her body was turned, like it had never been before in all the years she's been a resident here. I took no chances and reported it to security, Then I left a message on your voicemail."

"Did security here say they noticed anything out of the ordinary?"

"They haven't reported anything so far."

"Thank you Melony. First let me talk to Dora and then I'll need to speak to all the security people that were on duty at the time."

Walking away, Melony told him, "I'll see that they're ready when you want them."

Entering Dora's room Ernie was greeted as if nothing unusual had taken place.

"Ernest, my boy, welcome back to my little piece of heaven. Did you bring your lovely Julie?"

"She's awfully busy right now."

"Well, you tell her for me that life is too short. She needs to take time for herself."

"I'll do that." Gravnick changed the subject, "Melony told me you had a strange visitor earlier today?"

"Oh, it was nothing — just some prankster goofing around."

After a moment of hesitation, she continued, "It's like I told Melony — He was ugly as sin, never said a word, wore hospital scrubs, fit like a tent."

"Did you notice anything else unusual about the person?"

"Unusual like what? I'd say what I described was unusual enough."

"Did this person have any scars? What color was his hair? Long, medium or short?" Remembering the scene from the hospital tape of a fat aide struggling to get a patient into the back seat of a Buick at the ambulance loading area, Gravnick added, "Could the intruder have been a woman disguised as a man?"

"A woman? I've been thinking about him being so fat and all. I guess it could have been…hard to tell."

"Let me put it another way — would you swear under oath that it was a man?"

"When you put it that way, I'm not so sure."

"But why are you questioning me like this? It's like you know something I don't."

"Just a hunch. I need to follow up on something." Gravnick noticed Melony had gathered the security team in the lobby and told Dora he'd be back

Gravnick introduced himself. "I'll try not to keep you people very long. What I'm curious about is anything and everything you might have seen, heard, sensed or encountered in any way prior to, during or even some time after you were alerted to the disturbance in Dora Gravnick's room this morning?"

Gravnick prompted, "Anyone?"

One of the security guards held up his hand. "I was watching carefully both before Mrs. Gravnick's alert as well as afterwards and saw no one fitting the description of a fat, ugly looking guy dressed in aide's scrubs."

"Did anyone see this guy?" Ernie asked.

No one said anything.

Gravnick continued, "Okay, at any time shortly before you were made aware of the incident, as well as following the incident, did any of you see someone coming or going? In particular did you see anyone or anything out of the ordinary? Was there anyone one that stood out or that specifically got your attention?"

After a moment of silence, a man said, "Well, yeah. I remember seeing a woman come out. But it was some time after we got the alert. Like maybe thirty five minutes later."

"You saw a woman leave the building?"

"Yes, sir," the guard responded.

"Was she the only one you saw?"

"It was a slow morning. Nobody, except a few of the usual folks."

"Did you get a good look at the woman? Was she someone you recognized?"

"I got a good look at her. She was an absolute knock out. Didn't know her though. But, sure wish I did."

"Can you describe what she looked like? Tall? Short? Blond? Brunette? Redhead?"

"Yeah. Tall brunette.

With that two other security people piped up. They too had observed the same woman.

"She walked right past the front desk and offered a friendly goodbye on her way out the front door."

"She waved real sweet and cute. I agree, she sure was a looker all right."

Gravnick said, "I'd like to get a police artist down here. That is, if you can give enough details to provide a portrait. That be okay?" The group agreed.

Gravnick checked his watch and realized it was after hours. The portrait would have to wait until Monday. Prior to dismissing everyone he checked the security people's schedules to make sure they'd be available. Then Gravnick returned to Dora's room and spent the afternoon visiting his mother.

CHAPTER THIRTY-TWO

Monday morning Dilly's office had a peculiar smell. "It's bleach and something else — burned plastic maybe —" he told Ed Frankel, the desk sergeant.

"It's a mess inside that open safe," Ed said.

Gravnick stepped in front of Frankel and kicked the door to the safe shut with his heavy leather shoe. "That will keep the smoke and smell from spreading."

"Seems you left your safe open with something flammable inside," Sgt. Frankel said.

"I didn't leave it open," said Dilly. "I remember specifically putting the hospital tapes in and closing the safe up tight. Even gave the combination lock and extra whirl to make sure." Hesitating, Dilly added, "My office door was locked, as was the safe. Someone had to have gotten in here. You were on duty all night, Ed. Did you see anyone snooping around?"

"How many people came in here last night?" Gravnick said.

"It was a quiet night. As far as traffic through here, there were three, maybe four street teams checked in before going on duty and likewise checked out afterwards."

"Let's go over the time sheets of those on duty last night. That fire didn't start all by itself. Someone broke into that office and managed to crack the safe."

"You want me to get the time sheets for you, Chief?" Frankel asked.

"Yes."

Anxious to see how badly the tapes were damaged, Dilly reopened the safe, but slammed it shut again. The caustic stink made his eyes burn.

At the same time, Ed Frankel returned with the time cards and duty rosters. A quick review showed nothing out of the ordinary. Only the officers originally scheduled had signed in.

Gravnick said, "Look, Ed, before you leave, I want you to sit down and list everything you did while on duty here last night. Include a list of everyone that came in and everything any of them may have said to you. Even if they just said hello, goodbye, joked around or anything else."

"I think I already told all, but okay, I'll do the list."

"You told me only a few highlights. I want you to write it down. All of it. Every last detail. Like did you watch TV? If so, what shows did you watch? What were they about? Also, anything else that happened while you were watching TV. Any phone calls you received or conversations you might have had on the phone or with people that came in. You got that?" Ed nodded.

"While you're doing the recap, Dilly and I will get a couple of fans to air the place out."

Gravnick's secretary located a police artist for Gravnick and set up a session at the nursing home for two o'clock that afternoon.

Even before the police artist completed a composite sketch of the woman the security folks claimed to have seen leaving the nursing home, Gravnick's unspoken theory was proven. He glanced over the artist's shoulder, his eyes fixed on the woman he'd witnessed on the night of the fire-bombing at Bella Vista.

A few minutes later, the artist completed her sketch. It was the woman everyone had seen leaving the nursing home.

Gravnick thanked the security people for their time. Then, turning to the police artist, Gravnick told her, "I have another job for you."

His latest hunch had turned to a full blown itch that needed to be scratched.

Walking down the hall toward Dora's room, Gravnick explained to the artist what happened to his mother the day before. "The man she described to me sounded very much like the one that was in our hospital video." As they approached Dora's room, Ernie knocked on the open door.

"You're here on a Monday?" Dora said, "Did someone tell you I died?"

"No, Mother. I'm here on police business, hoping you might be able to help us."

"How can a dilapidated old broad help the police department?"

Gravnick chuckled. "I'd like you to describe the person who taunted you yesterday. Our artist might be able to draw a likeness of him."

"I hardly saw him. Just a fleeting glance."

"I know. Just tell her what you told me yesterday."

"Sure, like I've got something better to do." Then with a nod of her head to the artist, Dora quipped, "That's my son. I wouldn't tell him but he's awful cute, isn't he?"

The artist smiled. "I won't tell him if you won't. Tell me what you remember about the person? Was he tall?"

"Heaven's no." Dora said. "Short. And fat."

"Could he maybe have been of average height?"

"Maybe — average height."

"Are you sure it was a man?"

"My son asked the same thing. I thought it was a man, but I can't be sure of that either. On the other hand, no woman could have been that ugly. Except maybe me." She laughed.

"Come on, you're not ugly." The artist smiled. "What else can you tell me about him?"

"He was wearing a scrub suit, like the doctors and aides in a hospital. On him it was a tent."

When the artist was done, Gravnick studied the sketch, then turned to the artist and said, "Thank you so much. This will be a big help." He kissed Dora good bye.

On his way back to the station Gravnick answered his cell phone.

"Gravnick here."

"It's me, Moose."

"Moose? Oh, yeah. How are you?" He had never received a phone call from the man in all the years he had known him.

"You ask for something on a certain somebody," Moose said in a hushed voice.

"You're right, I did."

"Well, I got something. Might be good. Might be bad. I dunno."

"Can you tell me about it?"

"Yeah. But not on the phone. You want I come to you, or meet here?"

Remembering his promise to Jonathan to take him to the Chicago Police lab, he arranged to meet Moose at his place. He figured meeting Moose and Big John at the pool hall would be interesting to the boy. Afterwards he'd take him over to the Police Lab.

It was late afternoon when Gravnick arrived back at the Highland Park Police Headquarters. Circulating fans created quite a breeze. Much of the stink was gone.

Sampson and Jack Dilly were conversing outside Dilly's office.

"Looks like the fans really cleared the air," Gravnick remarked.

"Things are pretty much back to normal," Dilly said.

Sampson added, "Everything in the safe including the hospital tapes was reduced to sticky sludge. Too bad. I just wonder how…"

"We'll see Ed Frankel when he comes in tonight. Hopefully he'll remember something. In the meantime, I think we've got something useful."

"What?" Dilly asked.

"Seems the orderly that showed up on the hospital tape also paid a visit to my mother's room at the nursing home."

"Is that guy working at your mother's place now?" Sampson asked.

Gravnick shook his head. "Whoever he is, he apparently showed up for the sole purpose of harassing Dora. I haven't figured it out. Unless, he thought it would scare me off from investigating Julie's case. I don't know…"

"Is that it then?" Sampson questioned.

"There's more. Dora, God bless her, gave us enough for a good artist's rendering, including some facial features."

"Well, all right," Dilly said with a sigh. "Time we caught a break on something."

"That's not all. The security people at the home spotted a strange woman leaving the place shortly after the incident with Dora, and the police artist came up with a composite that fit their image and I swear she's the same woman I saw wandering around Bella Vista the night of the bombing."

"That's a bit of all right." Sampson said. "Hmm. Do you think maybe the woman and the fat guy could be one and the same?" That might explain why the guy had so much trouble getting whoever it was into the car at the hospital."

"That's what I was thinking," Gravnick said. "We've either got ourselves a quick-change artist, or a few people working together. In either case someone's targeting Julie and me. Who it is, I have no idea. Even more disconcerting, I don't know why."

"So where do we go from here?" Dilly asked.

"I'm going home. Since this whole thing broke with Julie I've hardly been around for Jonathan. We finally moved from the hotel into the house we're renting, while waiting for Bella Vista to be put back in shape. I hate for the kid to be there alone so much. Although he doesn't seem to mind, since he has his camera equipment and darkroom back. Anyway, call me later if Frankel comes up with anything we can use."

CHAPTER THIRTY-THREE

Gravnick and Jonathan were concentrating on a game of chess when Ernie's cell phone interrupted them. It was Jack Dilly.

"Yeah, Dilly, what's up?"

"Ed Frankel finished the assignment you gave him. He wanted to tell you himself. Okay?"

"Put him on."

"You were right, Chief. Writing everything down helped me remember that sometime late last night, I was watching a thriller on TV and I recalled, one of the guys came in and said 'Hello, Ed. How's the world?' I remember responding, 'it's been a quiet night' and he answered, 'Let's hope it remains that way.' But, I can't tell you who it was. Guess I was so into the movie, I must not have looked up. All I know is he went in the back. He was there for, maybe twelve or fifteen minutes, came back out, and I believe he said goodnight or some such. Then he left."

"Good, Ed. I'll be in later."

Earlier, Ernie had mentioned to Jonathan that he could skip school the next day, in order to accompany him to his meeting with Moose. "You can see where I worked when I was growing up. Then, we'll go over and take a tour of the Chicago Crime lab."

Jonathan said, "That's great. But I don't have to skip school. It's teacher's day. No classes."

"Well, good," said Ernie. "I was going to call the school in the morning to get you excused. Now I won't have to."

—✦—

Gravnick remembered Moose was always in his office by eight in the morning. Likewise, Big John would be in early to meet the delivery trucks bringing in supplies.

Ernie knocked. Big John opened the door. "Ernest me boy. And who does we got here?"

"John, this is my friend Julie's son, Jonathan."

"Hello, Mr. Big John, sir."

"Jonathan, is it?"

"Yes, Sir, Mr. John."

"Well, 'tis nice meetin' ya Master Jonathan — and welcome to our place. Now, come in. Come in. Yer don't want to just be standin' out there."

Jonathan stepped in first and was met by Big John's outstretched hand. "Put 'er thar, me boy."

Jonathan reached out to shake the big man's hand, and saw his own hand disappear into John's huge paw.

"Ah, yer got a good strong handshake, me boy."

"Ah, Ernest. Ernest. I hardly knows what to say. Don't sees ya for all them years, now here's ya are twiced in 'most a few days. 'Tis like a miracle from God."

"I'm hardly a miracle — and the only God around here is The Moose man, who asked me to meet him here."

"Suren, he did mention dat. But, me old head forgets. 'Tis a wonder these days"

"Yes sir, you are a wonder. That's why I love you, you ancient oaf." Big John gave Gravnick a suffocating hug. Gravnick broke free of the big man's embrace.

"Now, tell Moose I'm here — and keep an eye on Jonathan for me, while we talk. Okay?"

"Twill be me pleasure. Just, as me and you did in the olden days."

Moose came out to greet Ernie, "Figured was you. Who's the kid?"

"Moose, this is Jonathan, my friend Julie's son."

"D'ya need a job, son? Put you to work here, just like Gravnick done at your age."

"He doesn't need a job, Moose," Gravnick said. "We'll leave him with Big John."

"Come in back. We'll talk private," Moose said.

Moving to Moose's office, Gravnick took a chair in front of the large old desk. Moose dragged over another guest chair and sat directly facing him.

"What I got, is two things — and ya gotta understand — I dun' know, if they's for real or not."

"I understand," Gravnick replied.

"The first thing's Mr. Anthony Russo. A very hard man to learn 'bout. It's like nobody knows him. Nobody's talkin' 'bout him. How-so-ever, he owns businesses. Lots of them. The right kinds. They're all *wash* machines. You knows what I mean?"

Gravnick nodded.

"I'm thinking he's the main man for movin' drugs."

"In Chicago?"

"I thinks, for the whole country. Maybe more than the U.S."

"That big? Shee…it."

"Like I said, it's just from what I picked up." Gravnick stood up to go.

"Hold on, I'm not done. I told you I got two things, dint I? Again, I don't know if it's for real but, the talk going 'round is, there's this super-guy-hitman. Very 'spensive. They say he works all sides. Got no 'legiance to no one. Does his own thing. Who'e is," (he shrugged his shoulders) "nobody knows. Nobody's ever seen 'em. He's like a ghost person. But, they say he's real thorough. Does a very clean job. Leaves no trail."

"If he's what you're telling me, and nobody knows who he is — how do they communicate? How do they pay him?"

"Everything's up-front. Ya understand? They never done that. It's always been, part up-front. The rest, after proof of job done. So he's like a ghost. Nobody knows him, or has ever seen him."

"Thanks, Moose. I appreciate your help. I owe you."

"You'se owe me nothing." The two men shook hands and exchanged hugs.

Gravnick walked out to the main area, in time to catch the action at a pool table, where Big John was working with Jonathan, showing him how to improve his bank shot.

"I see Big John has you well on your way to becoming a pool shark."

"Aiy, Ernest. The boy 'as a good eye. 'Es goin' to be beatin' yore hide. Ya needs ta brings 'im 'round 'ere for practice."

"Mr. John showed me how to play eight ball," Jonathan said.

"Well, the Chicago Police Lab awaits us."

As Jonathan turned to say goodbye, he was smothered by one of the big man's hugs. Gravnick swallowed hard as he watched the boy's arms encircle Big John's bulky waistline. It reminded him of how it was with him, back in the day.

"Seems you've annexed another member to the family, Jonathan," Gravnick mused.

"Seems dat way, huh? Ya be bringin' him 'round now. Promise?"

"Promise." Gravnick shook the big man's hand, got, and returned, the crusher hug.

At the Chicago Police Department's Crime Lab. Jonathan found that, until the last few years, most of the ballistics and forensic testing for the Chicago Police Department, had been farmed out to the Illinois State Police lab. The turn-around time was often lengthy, taking days.

The new centralized forensic testing center that opened in 2013, also processes crime-scene photos for detectives and prosecutors, tests evidence for fingerprints, and prepares evidence for DNA testing. With a state-of-the-art crime lab, all under one roof, the amount of time to complete the various tests, had greatly improved. A ballistics test that might have taken days, in the past, may now be completed in a matter of hours, or even minutes.

Jonathan asked one question after the other and amazed the lab workers with his technical knowledge of camera types, exposure modes, pixels, image sensors, shutter speeds and lighting problems.

When their tour of the lab was over, Ernie and Jonathan drove back out to Highland Park. The boy, excited from the day's adventures, rattled on about the old pool hall, the fun he had with Big John, learning to shoot pool, and the sto-ries the big man told him about the old days. Ernie could hardly get a word in as, Johnathan continued on, about the Crime Lab, to rehashing the sights and fun he experienced at the pool hall. The trip back seemed to fly by, in-spite of fairly heavy traffic on the Edens. As they turned off the expressway, Gravnick asked, "Do you mind if we stop by the station, before going home? I need to check in."

"Okay." Then, with innocent sincerity Jonathan said —"Ernie, I really like doing things with you. You're more a real dad to me, than my father ever was."

These palpable words from a supposed introvert, moved Gravnick to tears — his eyes welled up, his voice caught. "Thank you Jonathan. I like you, too. And I totally like doing the things we do together."

CHAPTER THIRTY-FOUR

Gravnick and Jonathan pulled up outside the police station and spotted Sampson getting out of an unmarked department car.

"Hi, Chief. You guys just getting back from the city?"

"We are. Where are you coming from?"

"Dug up more dirt on Russo. He's into everything."

"Good. I got some interesting tidbits myself."

"Jonathan, hang in for a couple. I need to talk with Sampson and Jack Dilly."

"OK."

The men met briefly. Sampson reviewed his new finding on Russo. Gravnick checked his watch and decided, his report was too heavy-duty to get into at the end of the day. They agreed to meet again in the morning.

The following day Jonathan was off to school and Gravnick went to work, but concern weighed heavily on him. It was after ten o'clock when the three men came out of Gravnick's office, all of them down-in-the-mouth.

Gravnick was worried. His information needed to be shared with Chicago law enforcement, as well as state and federal agencies, and they would want to know where it all came from? He knew he couldn't reveal his main source — Willie the Moose Gavanno.

If Anthony Russo was key to the distribution of illegal drugs, even just for the Chicago metro, the FBI, Homeland Security and the Treasury Department, should be notified. If the man's arm stretched cross-country, there was no choice. Even if Gravnick kept the investigation tight and close, it would still eventually come out.

The so called Super Hit Man — the Ghost, might be considered outside of our purview." Gravnick's mind still wandered. "But, if our thinking's correct, that he, or she, is potentially a quick-change artist, and he could be a woman, or she could be a man, we are already, far out front on this one. No one, outside of our department, was investigating this. If we attempted to share what we believe, we'll be laughed out of town. They'd tell us, we're reading too many comic books. He decided — For now, we'll keep this in-house."

Gravnick switched to Russo. Even without Moose's in-put, we've got more than enough on the man to broaden the investigation, he thought. There's absolutely no need to bring up his discussions, or relationship with "The Moose."

It was time to make a call.

"Captain House, here."

"Hello, Charley, it's Ernie Gravnick."

"Uh, oh. When you don't address me as "Charley Horse" I know it's serious. What's up, old friend?"

"We need to meet. We've got something that could be huge. Others will need to be brought in, but I think it best if you and I speak first."

"Can you give me a hint as to what you're talking about?"

"All I can say on the phone is, it has to do with the drug trade."

"Okay. When do you want to do this?"

"I have to write this up first. How about later in the day? You live on the north side. We could meet somewhere in between — where we can have some privacy, get a drink — and I don't have to schlep back to the city again? Maybe the Evanston Country Club, on Dempster? Julie is a member. We can get in as her guest. I'll get us a small meeting room. About 6 o'clock, okay?"

"Sounds good. See you there."

Sampson and Dilly knew their assignments. Both were working, on their computers. Turning to his own computer screen, Gravnick began inputting the details of his presentation for Charley House. This was not something he could give to a secretary to handle. The other men's reports were also confidential.

Gravnick got to the Country Club early and cased the place out. By the time Charley came in, Gravnick had wandered back into the reception area and led him to the bar. They ordered drinks, then moved to a private room to discuss the Russo matter. Later they had dinner. Charley House expressed his surprise, when he first heard of Russo's probable involvement.

"This guy is so off the grid, we might never have suspected him," Charley noted.

They finished up with a plan for the two of them to move forward and agreed that Charley would set up a meeting with the Chicago Police hierarchy, and whatever other agencies they deemed appropriate.

"I'll let you know when the meeting is going down. They'll want you there, to address their concerns and answer questions — and there will be questions. By the way, you did right coming to me first. At least the two of us will be working the same plan. With a little luck we won't cross each other up." The entire time they were together neither man mentioned Julie Winton. It wasn't appropriate.

The sun swallowed up the last nighttime shadows as Gravnick pulled opened the door to Paul Diamond's reception area. It was too early for the receptionist and his gaze took in the English Gothic décor of the room, coming to rest on the half open entry to Diamond's private office. As he stepped across the plush carmine colored carpeting, Gravnick saw Diamond at his desk. He was deep in thought, hovering over a legal pad. Gravnick's gentle wrap on the door frame diverted Diamond's attention and he looked up, startled. "Chief Gravnick. Come in. Why didn't you let me know you were coming?"

"I was just driving by and thought I might catch you for a minute," Ernie said. Actually he had planned to surprise him.

"What I want, to know is exactly what you're doing and where you're going with the case against Julie Winton," Gravnick asked.

"Well, you know, it's a complicated case. I can't just lay it all out for you at the drop of hat. If you'd called and given me some time to prepare…"

"I should have called, so you could've jerked me around, just like you did with Julie. That game stops right now. So tell me, what's going on, Paul?"

"You're right, Gravnick. I have been stalling. Stalling for time. I've been so snowed under with cases, I've been unable to keep up on any of them. But, no more. We're going to get on with Julie's case right now — and if you have some time, we'll do it together. Okay?"

Before, Gravnick could answer. Paul, resumed speaking, turned around, stood up, walked to a row of file drawers, opened one, and while rummaging through it, kept talking.

"Actually, what I just said was not entirely true. After speaking with you last week, I've been thinking a lot about her case. He spread the file open, grabbed a pencil, began to write, and said; "Okay. Let's get on with it. Shall we?"

"All right. Tell me your plan for the opening statement."

Gravnick spent the next hour, going over the attorney's thoughts, throwing in a few ideas of his own, and watching Diamond write it all down. Finally, Diamond tried out a tentative opening statement.

"Good morning, ladies and gentlemen of the Jury. My name is Paul Diamond. I'll be representing the defense in this case, Julie Winton. Some of you are probably familiar with Miss Winton. You may have seen her on television. There is a good chance that you have even read about her, in a newspaper, or in any number of magazines. You might have even purchased one or more of the products her company produces. Possibly, you think you know quite a bit about her. But, do you really know Julie Winton? Over the period of this trial, I will attempt to help you get to know her better. To know who she really is. Not just in her public life, but in her personal life. When among friends and family.

"We are here today because Julie Winton has been accused of murder. Of brutally killing a man. A man, who himself was a known criminal. You will find out that, in order for her to have done this terrible deed, she would have needed to perform several near miracles. For example, she would of had to snuck out of the hospital room, to which she had just hours before been admitted. This was after barely escaping an assassination attempt. When brought into the hospital, technicians attached her up to all kinds of monitors and IV lines.

"Let me ask — how many of you have ever visited someone in a hospital? How many of you at one time or another, have actually been patients in a hospital? Okay. So then you have a pretty good idea of what it's like, being hooked up to all the monitoring equipment they use.

"It's pretty cumbersome, isn't it? Uncomfortable? Yes, and it certainly would not have been an easy feat to unhook yourself from. Would it? It usually requires the help of a nurse, or an aide. So, you would agree, that if Julie Winton had indeed shed all the monitoring lines and IVs by herself, it would have been a very difficult act to perform? Well, all the things I just mentioned, are exactly what the prosecution will try to have you believe the defendant did.

"But, let's just pretend, that in some miraculous way, Julie Winton had been able to do those things. She would then, have had to walk out of her room on the 7th floor, slipped past the nurse's desk, which was located directly across from her room. She would have then had to get past any nurses, doctors or other hospital personnel that were on the floor at the time. If she had gotten by all of them, without being seen, she would have next had to walk down seven flights of stairs or, alternately, have taken the elevator down seven floors to the first floor. Now remember, she would have had to do all of these things, without being seen or noticed by anyone.

"Again, let's pretend she performed these amazing feats. This is just the beginning of the performance the prosecution will ask you to believe. After getting this far, Miss Winton would have had to walk out of the hospital, go to the parking lot, and among all the many cars parked there, she needed to find one car, mind you — one car that was not locked. She would have had to hot wire the car, drive it out of the guarded parking lot, show the guard a parking slip — Go all the way into the city, to an address she had previously never been to — Get into the house, commit a brutal killing of a man, who was in top physical shape — wipe most everything clean that she may have touched, while committing this killing — then drive herself back the hospital in Highland Park. Put the car back in the exact same spot it had previously been parked, and then re-enter the hospital.

"But she wouldn't have been done yet. She would still have had to get back up to the seventh floor. Either by elevator or by walking up the stairs. Go back to her room. Hook herself back up to all the wires and IVs, and get back into bed. Oh, and again, do all of this, without letting anyone see her, or even realize she was gone. And there is one more thing, I almost forgot — during all this time, according to her doctors, Julie Winton was suffering from a severe case of shock, due to the earlier attempt on her life, from one or more persons, firing multiple automatic weapons into her car. Which by the way killed her longtime employee and friend Dylan Sullivan."

~✦~

Convinced that Diamond was on track to properly defend Julie, Gravnick left the attorney's office. Finding his way back through the maze of outer offices, he passed Paul's staff, who had by now arrived and were hard at work. It was also time for Gravnick to go to work.

CHAPTER THIRTY-FIVE

Before heading out of the city, Gravnick called Charley House. When he inquired if a meeting time with the powers that be had been set yet, he was reminded by Charley, of how slowly the bureaucratic wheels turned.

"Not to worry about having to drive back into the city today. I haven't been able to speak with anyone yet. My boss is out of town and if I'm lucky to catch him tomorrow, it won't be until late in the day. Figure a meeting won't take place 'til later in the week. It may even lapse over to the beginning of next week."

Gravnick pulled onto Interstate 94, Edens Expressway — so named for William G. Edens, an early 1900's Illinois banker and advocate for paved roads. Settled in for the ride back to the suburbs, Gravnick's thoughts keyed in on Moose's "super" hitman.

Could our so-called Ghost also be the quick change artist? Does the Ghost actually exist? Does the quick change artist exist? If either is real, how do we catch him/her? Where do we go from here? The old adage says — "When in doubt — Go fishing."

That's what we should do. Bait the hook, and reel 'em in. Another adage: The right bait catches the biggest fish. What, where, or who, do we use as bait?

Victims: Dylan Sullivan, Salvatore Giaconte, Jr., Julie Winton and Dora Gravnick.

The first two being deceased, narrows our choice to Julie and Dora. Though I would prefer not to put either of them in greater jeopardy.

Other possible victims: Jean Caron and me.

Places of suspect involvement: Belle Vista, Northshore University Hospital, Highland Park Police Headquarters, Anthony Giaconte, Jr's home and perhaps Geneva, Switzerland.

Which one offers up the tastiest lure?

Gravnick got to his Highland Park office and shouted, "Dilly. Sampson. In my office. We're goin' fishing…for a ghost." For simplification, he adopted Moose's "Ghost" to identify who they're looking for. He wanted their input on baiting the hook.

He explained his thought process; "Until proven otherwise, I suggest we treat *Quick-Change Artist* and Moose's *Ghost* as one and the same."

Sampson and Dilly nodded in agreement.

Sampson was first to test his ideas on the other two men. "We could get the word out that the lab discovered DNA taken from a hair sample found at one of the crime scenes. We say that it doesn't match either the victim's or that of the suspect, Julie Winton. It could have come from the car that Julie was purported to have stolen from the hospital parking lot. Or it might have been found at the Giaconte murder scene."

Dilly followed up with, "Other than hair, maybe a fingerprint showed up on a remnant from the bomb used at Bella Vista. Chances are, the perp, even if he wore gloves, would have needed to remove them, to set up the intricacies of wiring a bomb with an electronic remote detonator. Thus, the possibility of a fingerprint."

"Although we found nothing in your office, it's possible, whoever opened the safe in your office, wasn't wearing gloves or took them off when he cracked the combination," Gravnick added.

"How about the nursing home?" Sampson said, "if the aide your mom saw, changed into woman's clothing before walking out of the place, it's likely she went into a lady's room, a closet, or any vacant room, in order to change without someone seeing him/her. It's certainly plausible, even likely, that he/she took off any gloves and unwittingly left prints, or could easily have shed some hair while changing."

"All these things are possible," Gravnick said, " but will any of them lure the fish to the bait, or cause him to take the hook? I think not. We need something else. Something so revealing that the perp is willing to take a chance on getting caught. It's got to be something that he thinks might reveal his/her identity, or might in some way lead us to him."

"The hospital tapes," Sampson said. "That had to be the Ghost that did it.

Dressed as a cop, he came to the station and destroyed the tapes. I'd lay odds on it — and if he took the bait once, chances are he'd take it again. The story for us to put out is; we only had copies of the tapes. The hospital maintained the originals. We've asked for another copy. We'll also let it be known that we had viewed something unusual before the tapes were burned but hadn't had an opportunity to verify our suspicions yet. We believe the tape could help us nail this guy, whoever he or she may be."

"It makes sense," Dilly said. "But, whoever it was, called Ed Frankel by name…even if he had somehow gotten his name in advance…how did he know he was the duty officer assigned that night?" Dilly asked.

Gravnick considered, then said "We really haven't had time to question the "who" of the break-in. The thought hit me that it might have been an inside job. If not an actual employee, perhaps someone who got the information from one of our people, either by accident or on purpose."

"Then again," Dilly said, "if our Ghost is a smart as we think, there are other ways he could have found out. He might have simply called in for information and prior to hanging up, said "Thank you. You've been so very helpful. May I have your name? I'd like to write a note to your boss commending you."

"Could have been any of those and more." Gravnick agreed. "We'll investigate this internally to find if any of our people were involved. More important, Sampson's got it right. If the tapes brought him out once, it could be just what we need to make him bite again."

Gravnick went on with his reasoning. "Before we release any of this, it's imperative to notify the hospital folks, as well as alerting our own people. The suspect is more than likely to go straight to the source for the originals rather than trying to come back here again. "

"Will this create too great a danger for the hospital and their patients?" Dilly asked. "You're right Jack. My God…if the Ghost turned out to be the same guy responsible for the bombing at Bella Vista and/or the Police Headquarter building in Geneva, he could very well try to blow up the hospital and everyone in it just to destroy the tapes. We must be extremely careful to couch our story in a way that makes the Ghost believe we already have copies of the tapes. It's also essential we make him believe the originals have been moved from the hospital to an off-site storage vault. The hospital must not be put in danger because of us."

"Okay, Sampson, you write the first chapter of our "novel" for the Ghost. Jack and I will review it before it gets distributed. Let's hope we win a Pulitzer for it."

—◦◦—

Paul Diamond's secretary picked up on the first ring. "Attorney Diamond's office, This is Anna, how may I help you?"

Roy hesitated briefly —"Oh. I thought this was Mr. Diamond's private line."

"This is Mr. Diamond's phone, he's in conference right now. May I take a message and have him call you?"

After a short pause. "No, I think not. I'll call back."

"May I tell him who called?"

"Yes, you can. Tell him, his conscience called. That'll make him scream — don't you think?"

"I'm not sure, sir."

"That's all right. Just tell him."

"His conscience called. I'll tell him."

"The last Anna heard was the caller's laugh.

As Anna finished jotting up the message for Diamond, the door to his office opened. Anna handed him the odd message and returned to her desk.

Diamond glanced at it, then went back into his office without saying a word. He read the message several times. Then called out, "Anna, please come for a moment."

"Yes, Mr. Diamond."

"You spoke to the person?"

"I did."

"What did you think?"

"Well, he sure seemed weird. It didn't sound like a joke."

"Well, thank you...there's nothing else, Anna." Closing the door softly behind him, he walked back to his chair. Minutes passed. More minutes. Ever-so-slowly his chair began to swivel, as if willed by an unknown force — finally coming to rest at the sweeping view out his corner office window. He stared. The hour hand on the oversized wall clock behind him ticked on — another hour began.

Anna tapped lightly on his door. "We're leaving. Is there anything you need before I go?" No response. Everything went quiet — except for the tick of the big clock. The view outside darkened and faded to black. Tiny lights began to twinkle. With each passing moment, more lights tickled the darkness. Night leaked into the city at the same time the buildings began to glitter, as if millions of fireflies were present.

The phone rang. Diamond ignored it. The caller left a message… "Hello, Paul, I know you're there. Don't think you can ignore me. Remember my warning. I gave you five days extra to come up with a plan for how you are going to get Julie Winton to declare herself guilty to the murder of Giaconte. It's nearing the end of the third day … you have two days left … and you know what's going to happen to your family if your plan isn't successful. I can't wait to hear what you you've come up with, Paul."

Diamond listened to the entire message before he left for the day. Unlike the other times he'd heard the voice, this time it didn't bother him in the least. He saved the entire message and made an additional copy on his digital recorder.

At home that evening, Paul, Irena and the girls enjoyed dinner together. Angelia, their housekeeper, served up her famous recipe Jerk fish; Diamond's favorite island dish. He joked with his wife and laughed with his daughters, and had fun, something he'd missed for a long time. His career seemed to always get in the way. He was sorry about that. He always told the girls "Keep on having fun. No one knows how long any of this is going to be?" And now…

When the girls repaired to their rooms, Paul withdrew to his study where he worked late into the night. His cell phone rang several times. He ignored the call.

The following evening Gravnick came home from work home early. Since moving from the hotel to the rented house a few blocks away from Bella Vista, he had not yet hired anyone to care for the house and keep an eye on Jonathan. As a result that night they'd eat take-out again, as they had for the past several nights. Tonight would be Chinese he picked up from the little place around the corner from the police station. The food was better than most. He mentioned to Jonathan, "Remind me to call Jen Wooten at your mom's office. We need to have her find us some people to care for this place and get us back to healthy eating. Also, though you act older than your fourteen years, and in fact are perfectly capable of caring for yourself, I'll be in big trouble if Julie finds out that I've been letting you come home to an empty house after school." Agreeing with Ernie Jonathan said, "Mom's old fashioned when it comes to raising me. I guess it's not really so bad, though. It makes me know she cares."

Between them they devoured some hot and sour soup, an order of orange flavored beef, and an order of chicken in garlic sauce. Their meal over and the cleanup completed, Jonathan challenged Gravnick to a game of chess.

"Okay. I'll take you up on that, providing you're through with your homework."

"All done. Did it when I got home."

Gravnick's cell phone barked. Caller ID read: C. House.

"Hello, Charley. You have a meeting time for me?"

"No, I've got something else."

"So tell me — I've got to get back to beating Jonathan in a chess match."

"You'll be putting the chess game on hold for tonight."

"Why?"

"Seems that Paul Diamond left his office about 4 o'clock today."

"So?"

"It was the way he did it."

"I'm listening."

"Apparently, he put on his hat and coat, and walked right out — of his 18th floor office window."

"What?"

"Paul Diamond committed suicide this afternoon." Gravnick drew a deep breath.

"Paul Diamond is dead," Charley said.

"You're certain it was suicide? Could someone have pushed him — made it look like suicide?"

"We're certain. He'd been alone in his office all day. Came in this morning, carrying a Starbuck's coffee and his briefcase. His staff said he looked like he'd been up all night — told his girl to cancel all his appointments. He wasn't to be disturbed under any circumstances. The only contact he had after that was with his secretary. He asked her to bring him another coffee — also asked for a large corrugated carton. She asked him where she might find the carton he wanted. He told her to open up a carton of copy paper, empty it and bring it to him along with a roll of sealing tape."

"Was someone in his office while she was there?" Gravnick asked.

"She said she saw no one."

"Has his family been contacted?"

"Yes, the Coroner's office notified the family. They needed his wife to iden-tify the body. I figured you would want to be the one to tell Julie Winton."

"Yeah, thanks. I want to tell her in person."

"Ernie, there is something else we are going to need you for," Charlie added.

"What's that?"

"The corrugated carton that Diamond asked for — it's sealed and marked confidential and addressed to you. He also left a letter. It too, is addressed to you — marked For Your Eyes Only."

Gravnick drew another deep breath and let it out.

Then Charley said, "We're here in Diamond's office. Can you get down here now?"

"Let me make a call. I want to get someone to stay with Jonathan. Call you right back."

Gravnick turned to Jonathan, "They need me down town. I know you're okay on your own, but I don't know how long I'll be. I'd feel better if someone was here with you for the tonight." Jonathan shrugged his shoulders.

"Let's see if Sampson can come over." Gravnick dialed — spoke to Sampson — got a yes.

"That's good. I like Sampson — he'll take over the game for you — give me some real competition," Jonathan teased.

"All right, young man, if you're going to be smug, I won't let you win anymore."

"Yeah, sure."

CHAPTER THIRTY-SIX

Gravnick returned Charley House's call, to let him know he was on his way downtown.

"An officer will meet you at the front door. We've got the building on temporary lockdown. Only authorized people in or out until we're finished up here."

Half an hour later, Gravnick pulled up to a line of police barriers. Inside the barrier several squad cars were parked with a myriad of blue lights flashing. He rolled down his window calling to a nearby officer. The officer, seeing him, ran over, yelling at him to move his car out of the way. Flashing his badge, Gravnick explained that he's there on official business at the request Captain House. Satisfied, the officer moved one of the barriers and waved him in, telling him to park next to one of the squad cars. Told him, "Leave the keys in it."

Gravnick, pulled his car up, climbed out and headed for the row of glass doors, bidding entry to the building. There was police tape across all but one set of doors, so he knocked on the glass. The officer inside let him in. Gravnick said that he knew the way to Diamond's office and before the man could respond, Gravnick got in the elevator, the doors closed and the elevator lifted off.

Five minutes after arriving at Diamond's 18th floor office, Gravnick had read Paul's letter and was opening a separate directive that was attached.

After silently reading it through, Charley House inquired of Gravnick, "So?"

"It states that I am to open the carton and follow the instructions included therein. The carton along with its contents are to be opened in front of witnesses. He specifies the witnesses are to include, at least one ranking official of the Chicago Police Department, a criminal attorney, officially representing Julie Winton, a representative of the State Attorney's office, assigned to prosecute "the State of Illinois vs. Julie Winton" and a judge of the Criminal Court of Illinois."

"That's about as weird as it gets," Charley said. "It obviously has everything to do with the case against Julie Winton…but how does Diamond's suicide enter into this?"

"I guess the only way we're going to find out is by opening up the box," said Gravnick.

"And we can't open the damn thing without following his prescribed conditions," Charley complained.

"Seems like everything surrounding Paul's death and Julie's indictment is on hold, until we can fulfill his conditions," Gravnick said. "Which means we've got a lot to do, and do fast — before any evidence gets contaminated — before too much information gets out to the public — and before Julie Winton's case gets screwed up any more than it already has."

"Yeah," Charley House agreed. "We need to temporarily isolate this office. No one in or out without our say so. I'll put a man on guard here…taping it is not enough. The press — we'll have to manage what we give them. Tell them nothing regarding a tie-in with Julie Winton, other than her having been a client. That's public information. The coroner can move ahead with the autopsy. No problem there."

"Okay. But with all the people and departments involved, how do we keep this from leaking to the press? It's going to be like trying to plug up all the holes in a sieve as we're pouring water into it."

"I'll take care of the police department representative and notify the State Attorney's office." Charley told him. You handle Julie, get her an attorney — and see if you can come up with a Judge."

"Can do. We need to do this pronto. Like within the next 24 hours — or it's going to be a disaster," said Gravnick.

Early the next morning, Gravnick put in a call to Julie. After a considerable wait, while she was brought out from the cell, Ernie heard a guard yelling, "Winton. Phone call for you." A few moments passed before he heard her voice. "Hello. This is Julie."

"Honey, it's Ernie."

"Ernie, what's going on? Why are you calling me at this time?"

"I'm sorry, but I have to tell you that…Paul Diamond is dead."

"What happened? An accident? A heart attack?"

"No, it seems he committed suicide…late yesterday afternoon."

"Suicide? Paul wouldn't kill himself."

"I know. I can't believe it either. But from all indications, he was alone in his office for quite some time, made extraordinary preparations, which we believe include material regarding your case."

"You say, we believe, don't you know?"

"Not actually. We haven't been able to go through everything yet, but he left a note that leads us to believe your case may have played a major part in this."

"In what? What are you saying? He killed himself because of me?"

"We don't really know yet. All we know is he left directions, along with what we believe to be considerable material sealed in a box that, by the way, is addressed to my attention, to be opened only by me in front of specific witnesses."

"Holy Christ. I can't believe what you're saying. I sensed something was going on with him. I told you that he seemed vague about my case and was giving me the run around. But, killing himself…"

"I agree — and I don't know. What I do know is upon completing what he was doing in the office, he got up from his desk, put on his hat and coat and walked out of his 18th story office window."

"How horrible."

"Yes, it is. But, I need you to clear your mind for few minutes and listen. We've got things we must do. Foremost, we need to get you a new attorney. Is there anyone you want me to call?"

"Who can we call? Yeah, what's his name? I can't think — he did some work for us a while back — Jenn will know. Give Jen a call at my office. Ask her for his name and the name of his firm. They settled a wrongful death suit that had been filled against us. Did a great job."

"I'll do that. I was going to call her anyway. We need her to get us some help at the house. Just hope whoever the attorney is, he's not too busy to take on your case at this time. We need someone that can start immediately."

"Harry … Jacobs…That's his name. Jacobs, Smullian, Dott is the firm. I just remembered."

"That's good. I'll call him as soon as we're done here."

"In case Harry can't handle my case, ask him for a suggestion. I trust his judgment."

"I'll do that. I'll also call Jenn — she may know of another firm — she needs to be kept up to date anyways."

"You're right. Tell her I'll call when they let me. I need to go over some things with her. Poor kid, she's got the whole company on her shoulders right now. But, I know she'll handle it."

"All right. I'm sorry to leave you with all this, but time is of the essence. We need to get someone on your case and up to date as soon as possible. I also need to find a judge that can make himself available to us, so that we can carry out Diamond's requests."

Disconnecting his call with Julie, Gravnick began dialing 411 information. He asked for and got the number for Jacobs, Smullian, Dott. He let the service dial the number and send a text with the number to his cell phone.

"Hello…Jacobs, Smullian, Dott."

"Right. May I please speak to Harry Jacobs?"

"Who may I say is calling?"

"My name is Ernie Gravnick. Tell him I'm calling for Julie Winton."

"Just a moment, please."

Thankfully, Jacobs was available. The two men made plans to meet at Chicago Police Headquarters on Michigan Avenue at noon. Because of the sensitivity of the circumstances, Gravnick gave him only the necessary essentials.

Gravnick spent the next 40 minutes calling three different judges before nailing down one that could make herself available for later in the day. He then called Jenn Wooten — brought her up to date on Paul Diamond's untimely death — which she had already heard on the news. He explained that Harry Jacobs had been contacted and had agreed to take over Julie's case. Gravnick mentioned nothing more about Diamond. Changing the subject to Jonathan's and his need for help at the house — he asked Jenn to find people that will be able stay on for the long term —"For now and after we move back to Bella Vista."

By three o'clock all the necessary parties were gathered at the scene in Paul Diamond's office. Present were Captain Charles House, representing the Chicago Police Department, the Honorable Elizabeth Broddrich, Judge of the Criminal Court of Illinois, Fenton Capriccio, Assistant State Attorney, representing the prosecution, attorney Harry Jacobs, for the defense and Ernest Gravnick, who was there, not in his official capacity of Chief of Detectives and acting Chief of Police for the City of Highland Park, Illinois, but on behalf of the deceased Paul Diamond.

Charley House led off by introducing each of the parties and recapping the details of why they were all gathered there. He also explained that though we can all surmise as to why Diamond specified witnesses representing each of our professions, we are only guessing and should therefore try to keep an open mind until more is revealed to us. "With this in mind I'll have Chief Gravnick proceed. Thank you, Captain House…and thank you all for taking time from your schedules to be here under these rather unusual circumstances. I believe each of you had an opportunity to read the letter and separate directive Paul Diamond appears to have left behind."

They showed agreement with a shake of their heads or by saying yes.

"It seems we are ready to open the carton and see what mysteries are inside."

Everyone sat silently, as Gravnick picked up a box cutter he brought for the occasion. He carefully slit open the sealing tape, allowing the two top lids to partially open. After slipping the box-cutter into his pocket, he proceeded to bend the two bigger lids wide, then attacked the two side lids in the same way.

Gravnick spotted an envelope marked:

PLEASE OPEN AND READ ALOUD TO ALL ASSEMBLED

My name is Paul R. Diamond. I write this letter so that those of interest, may understand the circumstances of the past few weeks that have led to the taking of my life. I hope my dear wife Irena and my daughters will be able to forgive me and accept that what I have done is the only course I could have taken — in trying to prevent a terrible injustice — to honor the values I held dear and have lived by my entire life. But most of all — to save the lives of the three people I've loved most in this world.

Know that I have been living in a war zone. The actual battles have taken place within the gray matter inside my head. The combatants have been me — my values — everything I believe in — and the Devil himself. Imagine a tug of war. On one side is a force with their own absolute beliefs. The good guys. On the other — a force that holds exact opposite beliefs. The bad guys. No matter how hard they try, their differences are irreconcilable.

A few weeks ago I received a call from Jennifer Wooten of Winton Industries. She informed me that Julie Winton had just been arrested by the Chicago Police and charged with the murder of Salvatore Giaconte, Jr. Miss Wooten requested that I go to police headquarters as soon as possible where Julie was being held. She needed me to represent her at the arraignment.

Some twenty five minutes later, after pausing to pick up a copy of the indictment, I was standing outside a bank of elevators in the police headquarters building. The elevator doors opened and out walked Julie Winton with two officers escorting her. I had a few words with Miss Winton and the officers, who I also knew. They informed me that they were taking her to booking. I told Julie I would meet up with her as soon as they were finished.

Waiting for the elevator to take me to the visitor's center, where I was to meet with Miss Winton, I began to re-read the indictment. Having flipped through it when I first arrived, the charges seemed ludicrous based on the evidence. Perusing it again, I smiled to myself, thinking *the State's case is full of holes. This should be an easy win for me...A cinch to keep my unbroken record alive.*

As the elevator arrived, my cell phone rang. Automatically answering it, I was met by a strange voice, the likes of which I would never forget. "Mr. Diamond, I'm so glad you answer your own phone...that makes it so nice...don't you think?" the man stated in a high pitched, threatening way. Not only the voice but the words he spoke, burned indelibly into my memory.

Even so, I first thought it was a crank call, and was about to shut the phone off, when the caller mentioned my family. He threatened to kill them if I didn't do exactly as he demanded.

My immediate reaction was to get angry and threaten back — at which the caller upped the ante — telling me he was hanging up — and insisted I call my wife's cell phone. The phone went dead. He had gotten my attention.

My hand began to shake as I dialed my wife's phone. My whole body started to shake when her phone was answered by the same foreboding voice that had just hung up on me. "Hello again Mr. Diamond...or may I call you Paul?... Yes that would be much better," he said. Somehow, I can remember every word he said to me.

When he finally put my wife on the phone and I heard her pleading, I knew I had no choice, but to do exactly as he told me.

His instructions were quite clear. "You are about to lose the first case of your illustrious career — in fact you will make certain your client's case never comes trial. Julie Winton is to plead guilty to the charge of murder in the first degree for the killing of Salvatore Giaconte, Jr."

How he knew that Julie had been arrested or that I would be representing her, remains a mystery to me. I had gotten word of her arrest within minutes of her turning herself in and agreed to represent her just half-an-hour before receiving his call. I'd told no one. How this person could have found out — as I said — it's a mystery.

He told me that if I did as they say, my wife and daughters would not be hurt. When I arrived home that evening I found them there. They had been released — but, I had been warned — they could be taken again at any time. He made me believe they were constantly watching. Police protection or sending my family away could not save them. As you might imagine, my family was extremely upset and afraid. To allay their fears, I lied. I told them that I had contacted the police and that all would be okay. My family can verify what happened to them.

In the meantime my client had been calling — asking — no — demanding to meet with me. She wanted to know how I was going to defend her. I mostly stopped taking her calls. I was torn, not knowing what to tell her. It was not like me. But, I had no choice. The threat to my family was real. Coincidental to Julie Winton's demands and on her behalf, I endured tough questioning from her close friend Chief Gravnick, both over the phone and in personal meetings. Miss Winton and Chief Gravnick, please accept my deepest apologies for the way I treated you. You deserved better.

Worst of all has been the unending pressure of my own sense of guilt — to honor the oath I took to uphold the law — to be true to my personal values of truth and honor, verses giving in to the blackmailer's demands.

Over the next weeks calls from him came to me at any hour of the day or night. Constantly reminding and threatening. He let me know that the people he represented were getting impatient. Last week I was given a deadline — five days to get Julie Winton to plead guilty or my family would die. Tomorrow is the last day. I began taping the blackmailer's calls.

Here is a transcript of the tape:

"Hello Paul, I know you are there. Now don't you go and get a silly idea in your head that…etc…I gave you five extra days to come up with a plan to get Julie Winton to declare herself guilty to the murder of that awful Salvatore Giaconte, Jr., and you know what's going to happen to that wonderful family of yours if your plan isn't satisfactory to us."

Transcript finished.

Thanks to Chief Gravnick's urging, I wrote an opening statement, though at the time, I felt certain, I would never present it in court.

Your Honor, I ask you and the others assembled here to listen — and to allow this recorded statement, as well as the forgoing material, to be admitted into the record as evidence in the case of "The State of Illinois vs. Julie Winton."

At this point, Gravnick played Diamond's recorded statement fully exonerating Julie Winton. The document ended with the following closure:

Thank you, your Honor, for listening and for your consideration of my arguments and the evidence I have herein presented. Further I wish to thank all of you, for your time and indulgence. I know that this has been a highly unusual forum and perhaps not entirely legal under the law. Unfortunately it is the best representation I am able to provide my client under the circumstances. It must also be assumed that should this case go forward with other representation for Miss Winton, the unknown black-mailer will very likely continue to intercede.

With the tape concluded, Gravnick recapped; "There you have it — in Paul Diamond's own words — the apparent torment and soul-searching he must have gone through — the outrageous pressure, some of which we heard from the blackmailer's own voice, that had been put upon Paul Diamond, by him — whoever he might be — the pressure Diamond must have put upon himself, in order to stay true to his to his own sense of honor and values, his love of family — and as an officer of the court, to live up to his oath to uphold the law under unbelievable circumstances — all this he experienced on his way to making the ultimate sacrifice."

"Thank you, Chief Gravnick," Charley House said, as he stood up and walked over to where Gravnick was standing. Gravnick nodded and stepped away.

"Your, Honor," House said, looking to Judge Broddrich, "Would you care to give us your impressions of what we just witnessed — and in particular of how we might proceed from here?"

A refined looking woman in her 40's, Elizabeth Broddrich, was serving her fourth year of a six year term on the bench. In the short few years since being elected to the Illinois bench, she had gained a reputation as a tough but, fair-minded jurist. And now she spoke out clearly.

"First of all, Captain, I want to thank you and Chief Gravnick for the efficient manner in which you organized, as Mr. Diamond so aptly put it, this highly unusual forum. What we have heard and seen here today, not only seems to reveal some very upsetting and highly illegal happenings, but outright crimes. If all of this is true, we have acts of blackmail against an officer of the Court of the State of Illinois, three accounts of kidnapping, one or more acts of fraud and perhaps false imprisonment… and God knows what other threats. Not to mention a suicide. As this situation involves an ongoing murder case, before any decisions are made, I believe we need to hear from representatives of the prosecution and the defense. First, Mr. Capriccio, you've been witness to all that we have heard — may we hear from you?"

"Your Honor, indeed if we are able to substantiate all, or most of the information just presented, it may offer some consideration as to how we prosecute this case — though I do not believe it will alter our overall thrust. We will certainly need some time to fully review everything. Thank you, Fenton. Mr. Jacobs, I believe this case is new to you?"

"Yes, your Honor."

"I assume you will at least require some time to bring yourself up to date — and in lieu of this new information to consider how you will want to proceed?"

"Yes, your Honor," Harry Jacobs answered. "But from what little I already know about Ms. Winton's case, if what we heard here can be verified, I believe I can be ready to discuss any further action by noon tomorrow."

"Thank you, Mr. Jacobs. Well, then, unless there is something Captain House or Chief Gravnick wish to add…"

Charley House answered, "No, your honor."

Gravnick made a motion indicating he had something to say.

"Your Honor, the Highland Park Police Department has been doing an independent investigation of its own and has uncovered what we believe to be crucial evidence in Julie Winton's case. As there has been no time to present this information to either Ms. Winton's attorney or to Mr. Capriccio, and as this material could be critical to any action this forum may take, I would ask her Honor's permission to offer it into any further discussion."

"All right Chief. I believe that would be in order…and as we all have much to consider and will require some time for review, I suggest we adjourn now and meet again tomorrow at, say, 3 p.m. in my chambers."

CHAPTER THIRTY-SEVEN

After the meeting at Diamond's office broke up, Gravnick headed over to see Julie before visiting hours were over. He brought her up to date on their meeting and on what had been happening at home with Jonathan and him — also, that he spoke to Jenn about hiring a staff for the house. Gravnick went on to explain, "I don't want to get your expectations up, but you need to know that because of the things Diamond was able to bring out, there is a chance the case against you just might be dismissed."

"You mean I could get out of here?" Julie questioned excitedly.

"It's possible. But any number of things could screw up the outcome. So, let's not count our chickens just yet. But I want to say, if we don't get you out of here soon, I'm going to be a very unhappy guy."

"Why? What's going on?" Julie inquired.

"Well…because…damn it, I miss having you around. I'm finding that I really need you in my life."

"Wow, can I get that in writing?" Julie exclaimed.

"I'm being serious. Honest, this has never happened before. I've never needed anyone. I could always handle whatever came along. But, since you've been away — in this place — you're all I think about. I…I just need you. I guess…I guess I love you."

They both placed their palms up — hand-to-hand on the glass partition that separated them. For the moment, nothing more needed to be said.

A voice suddenly shouted her name and exploded their reverie.

"Winton. Your attorney is here to see you." A guard said.

"Upstaged by an attorney," Gravnick said. He threw Julie a kiss, and left.

Walking from the visitor's area, Gravnick spotted Harry Jacobs. "I gave Julie a general run down on our meeting — mentioned the possibility of the case being dropped — told her not to get her hopes up too high."

"Okay, I'll touch on it but, we need to approach it like we're going to go to trial. I have no idea of what is going to come down tomorrow. It could go either way. Maybe we'll get lucky."

Gravnick said, "Let's hope."

Next morning, at the Highland Park Police station, Gravnick and Jack Dilly read over a draft of Sampson's news release, with which they hope to target the Ghost. With a couple of minor suggestions, they signed-off and discussed where they wanted it placed. Gravnick reminded Dilly about notifying the people at the hospital about what they were doing.

"It's been done. They're good with it. More important, they found another security tape. You need to see it before you leave."

"Good. I'll look after we finish up here. In the meantime, are all our people clued in on what to watch for once we bait the hook?"

"Everyone's on it, Boss," said Dilly.

"Are any school tours, or any community events scheduled? They all need to be cancelled. We don't want anyone around that isn't supposed to be here. All strange faces, are suspects to be questioned…and make certain someone is on guard outside the building at all times. We don't want this place blown up like in Zurich."

"We have it all covered. Everyone's on board. We'll be looking for whatever and whoever — man, woman or beast," Dilly assured him.

"Okay, we're done here. Let's look at the security tape."

"This came from the hospital emergency area later that same night. It seems to nail down our theory of what happened. I think you'll want to take it with for your meeting later today."

As three o'clock approached, all concerned gathered outside of Judge Elizabeth Broddrich's Chambers. At three p.m. the door opened and Judge Broddrich bid them entry. After everyone was seated, she welcomed them and suggested the order for the day.

"First, you should know that after what we learned yesterday, I asked Captain House to speak with Mr. Diamond's family and if they verified the hostage-taking, to provide them with 24 hour security until everything is resolved. They verified the entire story just as Mr. Diamond related it. It is our belief that whoever is behind this could take revenge."

"Before we adjourned yesterday, Chief Gravnick indicated that his department had uncovered what he described as crucial evidence in the State of Illinois vs. Julie Winton."

"Mr. Capriccio. If the defense has no objection, I would suggest we allow the Chief to proceed with his presentation."

"I have no objection at this time your honor. But, as we have no idea what this so-called evidence is, I wish to reserve the right to revisit this later."

"Understand. Alright then, Chief Gravnick, please tell us what you have?"

"Thank you, your Honor.

"Though, those of you, less familiar with Julie Winton's case, have been brought up to date by Paul Diamond's narrative — I'll nevertheless, remind you that Ms. Winton had been hospitalized prior to being arrested for Sal Giaconte, Jr's murder.

"Knowing that, the Highland Park Police department, under my direction had reviewed the hospital's security tapes for the time period Miss Winton had been a patient there. What we found, leads us to believe that her thumb print and D&A could have easily been placed on the baseball bat at the crime scene by someone else. Specifically — the real murderer.

"Unfortunately, I am unable to show you the actual tapes — with the exception of one. The others were purposely and specifically destroyed, by someone who broke into our evidence safe. Mind you, those tapes were the only thing destroyed. I must therefore ask you to rely on my sworn oath to uphold the truth and integrity of my office — that what I tell you is to the best of my knowledge, the truth. I also believe that the one tape we do have, which fortunately for us, the hospital had somehow originally omitted, will be proof enough to back up our claim. May I proceed your honor?"

"Please continue, Chief."

"Thank you. As a preface to explaining what the tapes showed, we as well as the Chicago police had questioned the hospital staff, who had been on duty during the time in question. We know that from just after 1:00 a.m. until 4:30 a.m. no one remembered seeing Julie Winton in her room. We were told that just before 2:00 a.m. a code blue had been called and the staff was frantically busy trying to save the patient. As a result a couple of hourly check-ups were skipped by the night nurse."

"Ms. Winton told us that a nurse did check her at 1:00 a.m. At 16 minutes after one, just as she had started to doze, she said an aide came in to take her down for an MRI — she remembered checking the time and thinking — sleeping in a hospital was impossible. Annoyed, she told him she already had an MRI. He told her that there was something wrong with the first pictures and the doctor had requested another. Julie said she remembered nothing after that until a tech person came in at 6:30 AM to take blood. She was able to tell us the aide was fat to the extreme — obese, and had a Spanish accent.

"What got our attention in the hospital's security tapes, was an extremely heavy-set aide pushing a gurney with a patient, outside of the hospital in the ambulance drop-off & pick-up area. At the time, there was no ambulance, or EMT personnel around, only the gurney with a patient and the overweight aide. Parked in the ambulance area was a dark blue Buick sedan.

We were then able to view the aide as he struggled to lift the patient from the gurney and literally squeeze, the patient's limp body into the back seat. The time exhibited on the tape was 1:45 a.m. We were able to identify the car as a 1998 Buick, La Sabre. It had a Wisconsin license plate, number 356 196. We were unable to see the year on the license. However, it turned out to be the same car reported missing from the hospital parking lot later that night — it mysteriously turned up later that same morning, in the same space it had been taken from. Prior to the aide getting into the car and driving away, he rolled the gurney back and hid it under a staircase."

"As I said earlier, days later the hospital found another tape from later that same night that somehow had been overlooked. With Captain House's help, we'll view that tape now."

Charley turned on the video. "You'll note it shows the same aide returning — picking up the gurney he had hidden away — rolling it back to the car — pulling what looks like the same patient from the car — placing her back on the gurney—returning the gurney to his hiding place under the stairwell — this time leaving the patient on it. He then runs back to the car — drives away —presumably, from what was reported the next morning — re-parked it in the exact space he had taken it from. Walking back a few minutes later, we see him pushing the gurney with the patient back into the hospital. The time on the tape was 4:50 a.m. — Three hours and five minutes from the time we first viewed the aide putting the patient in the car. Actually, a little longer than the police originally thought Julie Winton was missing from her room."

"Nevertheless, we believe the patient on the gurney was Julie Winton. That the aide, or whoever he was, came to Ms. Winton's room. Sedated her. Took her from the hospital. Drove to the murder scene. Put her thumb print on the bat. Retrieved a sample of the earlier regurgitated food from Julie's hospital gown, and placed it on the bat. Voila — the perfect murder."

"Thank you, Chief. Mr. Jacobs, do you have anything you wish to add from the perspective of the defense?"

Harry Jacobs, who had been sitting quietly, stood up and alternately facing Judge Broddrich and Fenton Capprico said, "Yes your Honor…indeed I do. After everything we have seen and heard these past two days, I believe that without a scintilla of doubt, the state's case against my client Julie Winton has been proven to be based on a fabrication of evidence and is totally without merit. For these reasons, I ask that all charges against my client be dropped."

Judge Broddrich looked to Fenton Capriccio, who for the past several minutes had been nervously wriggling in his chair: "Mr. Capriccio, I take it you wish to respond?"

Jumping up, Capriccio waved his arms and began to sputter. "Oh, yes I do your Honor. Really, this whole procedure over the past two days has at best, been highly unusual. At worst, I'm not even sure it's been legal. What have we actually witnessed here — and what do we end up with? I say; *garbage*. It's been nothing more than a dog and pony show.

"Before yesterday we had an airtight case of first degree murder against Julie Winton. Now, what do we have? The rantings of a suicidal maniac, a recorded phone message that anyone could have made, and mostly hearsay from a very biased witness.

"The only real thing of substance was a hospital security tape that showed what seems to be, and I agree, the highly unusual actions of a fat person dressed like a hospital aide, dragging something wrapped in a blanket, out of a car, putting it on a gurney, rolling it aside, disappearing, reappearing and pushing whatever, or whoever is on the gurney into the emergency door. It proves absolutely nothing… and changes nothing." Having made his point, Capriccio sat back down.

"Well, it seems we have an opposing view," exclaimed Judge Broddrich. "Rebuttal — Mr. Jacobs?"

Rising slowly from the small love seat he'd been sitting on in the judge's chamber, Harry Jacobs' face broke into a broad grin. "Your Honor, I have to hand it to my colleague — he is certainly proving himself to be a master of the simplistic — but, simplistic is not realistic. I'll try not to take too much time, as we are all busy people — but, I believe a quick review of what we have heard and of what we know is in order. Paul Diamond drew us a clear and colorful picture of what went on prior to and during the time Julie Winton had been a patient in the hospital. His words were not, and are not, the ramblings of a sick, or suicidal person. Rather, they are those of a studied and practical professional. Though, admittedly, under extreme circumstances, what he set before us is still a completely logical assumption based on fact and circumstance. Nor, can we disregard the kidnapping of Diamond's family members. That was absolutely real and set up an ideal situation for blackmail. Even if we are only able to believe 50% of everything else we heard about, or saw in connection with Julie Winton's highly unusual hospital adventures — we must admit — there is no case — I do not believe there to be a jury, anywhere, that would not acquit."

"Thank you, Mr. Jacobs. And Mr. Capriccio, I believe you owe Chief Gravnick an apology. Though, I only met him two days ago, his reputation as a man of integrity is legend in this city. To infer that the information he related to us is other than the truth, one need be severely biased."

"Comments — anyone?" Judge Broddrich questioned.

Silence pervaded the chambers.

Humiliated and beaten, Fenton Capriccio stood up and looked at the judge. "You're right your Honor." He turned to Gravnick. "I do owe you an apology, sir. I was entirely out of order. On behalf of myself and the State Attorney's office, I humbly, ask your forgiveness. It seems, my frustration with this case, got the better of me."

Gravnick, barely speaking, accepted, waved his arm and offered a positive nod.Capriccio, turned back to Judge Broddrich. Your Honor, I also ask that the court accept my full apology for my actions."

"Accepted, Mr. Capriccio."

"As there are no further comments, I assume we are in full agreement with Mr. Jacobs. In the case of the State of Illinois vs. Julie Winton, I therefore declare this case dismissed for lack of evidence. Miss Winton is to be released at the earliest possible time. Captain House, if you will get Miss Winton's release papers to me — I will sign them."

CHAPTER THIRTY-EIGHT

After leaving Judge Broddrich's chambers, Charley House and Gravnick walked out to the plaza at the Richard J. Daley Center. Charley received a call on his cell phone and motioned Gravnick, to hold up a moment. The call was from his boss from whom he learned the joint meeting with the FBI, Homeland Security and the Chicago Police Department would convene at 2 p.m. the following day. The presence of Chief Gravnick was also requested.

After the call, the two men stood together staring out on West Washington St. At that time of the afternoon, the area was rife with traffic, both on foot and motor vehicle. It was early November. The sun was already beginning to set and a cold wind bounced off the steel and concrete buildings that aligned the street. Ernie pulled the collar of his trench coat high, half burying his face to ward off the biting cold. "How soon can you get Julie's release papers over to Judge Broddrich?" he asked.

"She'll have them soon. A clerk has already readied the paperwork and a messenger is on the way to the court house as we speak. I know you'd like to take Julie home tonight, but we need to follow protocol. If we don't, someone's going to get their head out-of-joint, and make it more difficult for us. I'd say the soonest we get her out, will be sometime tomorrow."

"Can we get a message to her to let her know what's happening?"

Looking at his watch Charley shrugged his shoulders. "The place is ready to go on lockdown for the night. I really don't want to pull rank at the last minute like this. As I said — it's best we follow protocol. If you can get down here first thing tomorrow, we should be able to settle everything by noon — before our meeting."

Not particularly happy with Charley's answer, Ernie ventured, "Sampson can pick her up when she's ready to go home."

The two men went their own way. Each headed into rush hour traffic out to the north shore suburbs. Each man contemplated what changes, the next day's happenings would bring to his life. In their profession, what other people did, can have significant impact on their life.

Gravnick had already experienced the changes brought about by his relationship with Julie and Jonathan. As he drove into the night, he thought about how, tomorrow's meetings with the Feds and City police officials might go. At the very least, the bar would be raised substantially.

The next morning, after everyone had been notified and all necessary paperwork had been filled, Gravnick waited in Charley House's office for word of Julie Winton's release. In lieu of what Paul Diamond had brought up about the mysterious blackmailer, and with the potential trap Gravnick and his people had set for the Ghost, Ernie decided to broach the subject with Charley.

"There is a theory my department is working on that you will need to consider as well. The blackmailer that haunted Diamond these past few weeks, we believe may be connected in some way to the mysterious hospital aide we talked about, and viewed on the security tape. Even more than that, we believe the person that set the bomb at Julie's Bella Vista home and set fire to the hospital security tapes at our station house, may be one and the same."

"That's kinda spooky. What brings you to that conclusion?"

"Actually there's more. We believe the aide that appeared on the security tapes from the hospital, is the same guy that showed up at my mom's nursing home and spooked her."

"What you're saying is, this guy gets around."

"That's only part of it. We're also thinking that the perp could be a very talented quick-change artist, capable of being a somewhat short, fat hospital aide one minute and a tall, slender femme-fatal the next."

"Come on. What kind of *B.S.* are you trying to feed me?"

"It's not bullshit. Hear me out, Charley."

"Okay, I'm listening. Tell me about your spook."

Gravnick continued. "After the incident at the Deerfield Nursing Home, their security people reported seeing a woman walking around, leaving the place, saying goodbye and driving out of the parking lot. One of them even thought, she gave him the finger when she left. What's more, the description they gave the police artist, seemed to be the same woman, I spotted hanging around Bella Vista the night of the bombing."

"As I said, she, he, or it... sounds like a spook."

"We call him *Ghost*...but *Spook* certainly works as well. Anyway, let me continue."

"There's more?" Charley House asked.

"I'm beginning to believe that this so-called spook may well be responsible for the shooting at Bella Vista, and the aborted hit-and-run on Jean Caron and me in Geneva — and if we can put him there — the bombing of Geneva Police Headquarters, and the taxi attack on me become very probable. He could be the one that's responsible for all of it, including shooting up Julie's limo, killing Dylan Sullivan and wounding Julie."

"So what you're trying to tell me is, you think we have a kind of super hit-man character, right out of the pages of a comic book?"

"I know it sounds corny, but, yes, it's exactly what I believe."

"Let me ask you — am I to believe the spook, or whatever, is responsible for all these terrible things...not only here...but, potentially world wide? I don't believe I'm even talking to you about this. Oh, hell. You're serious. Let me put it to you this way — all that being what it is, the one crime that seems our spook is likely to have committed — you haven't even mentioned — the murder of Sal Giaconte, Jr."

"I did say it. Well, maybe not in those words. But, in my explanation of the tape, I said it was my belief that while he had Julie, he managed her finger print on the bat and got her DNA from the dried regurgitation on her hospital gown — the perfect murder."

"Yes you did. I forgot — Okay, if he did these things, why did he do them? Did you or Julie, or Giaconte, or Jean Caron, or Dylan Sullivan do something to set him off? And, what about, Paul Diamond?"

"I can't think of anything any of us could have done. Hell, none of us have any idea who he is. And my Mother — she certainly did not have any contact with this guy prior to him showing up at the nursing home."

"So again?" Asked Charley House. "People just don't do these kinds of things without a reason?"

"That's right. They're either sick, revengeful, or someone's paying them. It's my belief that we are talking about a hit-man. And, no hit-man I've ever heard of works on his own — he works for somebody — it's the somebody he works for that we need to be thinking about. Actually, the guy on Paul Diamond's voice-mail mentioned "The people I work for…""

"You're right. He did," Charley remarked. "You know, that was a hell of an exercise we just went through. I guess we have to find ourselves a hit-man and the people he works for."

"Yeah. Just thought you'd like something else to think about besides Mr. Russo."

Looking at his watch, Gravnick said, "It's been over an hour. Can we find out what time Julie will be released? I need to let Sampson know what time to pick her up."

"They should have something by now." As Charley was about to grab the phone, it rang. "Captain House." He listened. "Yeah. Eleven. Okay. We'll have someone there to meet her." He hung up. "You heard? Downstairs, eleven o'clock."

—⋑◎⋐—

At eleven o'clock, Julie walked out dressed in the same street-clothes she wore, the day she turned herself in. Gravnick greeted her. "Have to say, you look a lot better in your own clothes, than in a prison jump suit."

"I kind of liked the jumpsuit — but, I don't ever want to wear *electric orange* again." Now, if you don't mind, I'd like to get as far away from this place, as soon as I can."

Ernie and Julie embraced. "I don't blame you," Gravnick said. "Unfortunately, I have to stick around for a meeting that could take some time. Sampson will drive you home."

"I get it. As an ex-con, my new mode of transportation is to be a squad car. Why not? I couldn't ask for a better chauffeur. Come on Sampson, let's go." Julie turned to Gravnick for a moment, and with both hands, pulled his head down, and gave him a tempting kiss. "Are you sure you don't want to come along?"

"You certainly make it tough for a guy to say no, but I can't. Save it for me until later."

"We'll see about that …"

—⋑◎⋐—

Roy heard the news of Paul Diamond's suicide on TV shortly after the police had released the name of the deceased. It came as a complete surprise. *Damn it. I had him right where I wanted him. Dangling like a marionette, on the end of a string, waiting for me to make him dance. Seems, I underestimated the dude. He figured a way out — clever. On-the-other-hand — not so clever. He's dead.*

—⊙⌒—

The remainder of the afternoon was swallowed by a grueling, time-consuming meeting of local and federal law enforcement's finest — or, shall we say, the top brass on both sides, pissed away the entire time, jockeying for position — trying to figure out who should report to whom, and about what. After all the farewells and goodbyes were completed, Gravnick asked Charley House, "Do you have any idea of who's supposed to do what and to whom?"

"Yes, absolutely. You and I will continue to do just what we've always done, until we nail Russo — or not."

CHAPTER THIRTY-NINE

Gravnick parked his car in the driveway of the temporary home they had rented in Highland Park. He honked the horn, to alert Julie of his arrival. Ernie pictured her waiting for him — being alone together, for the first time in these many weeks. He looked forward to a pleasant family dinner with Julie and Jonathan — spending the evening relaxing, and yes, later he and Julie would make love, and the woes of the past days would be swept away, as their minds and bodies melded in a state of bliss.

That was the mural Ernie had painted in his mind's-eye, as he stepped through the front door and was greeted, not by Julie, but rather, Jonathan, who proceeded to whitewash the image of his dream.

"Mother is upstairs packing. She received a call and has to go to Washington, D.C."

"Is she okay? What happened?"

"Grandma Jennifer had a severe heart attack, and while administering CPR to her, Grandpa Harry was stricken with a stroke. They're alive, but critical. The doctors are not certain either of them will last, until Mom gets there."

"Oh, God. Everything comes at once. Poor kid, she can't get a break. Are you okay?"

"Yes, I'm fine. Go be with her. She's going to need you."

Gravnick mounted the stairway, two steps at a time. As he entered the bedroom, Julie took the clothes she had piled on the bed, and folded them into the open suitcase, next to them.

"Hey, Honey. Jonathan told me about Jennifer and the Senator. I am so sorry," said Ernie.

"I know — guess life is not about to let us relax at any time soon," Julie responded, tears in her eyes. She turned to meet Ernie's full embrace. "I called Jenn — she'll take care of things on this end. My plane is being fueled and will be ready to take off, as soon as I get to the airport. She's sending one of the girls from the office over, to see that you guys have what you need."

"Can she stay with Jonathan? I'm going with you."

"That's not necessary, you're in the middle of everything with your cases. I can handle it."

"There is no way I'm letting you go by yourself. I'll pack a bag and be right with you."

Julie kept on trying to dissuade Ernie — however, her powers of persuasion faded. For the first time since she could remember, Julie felt unsure of herself. She had no idea how she would react, when faced directly with the possible passing of the two people who raised her, helped educate her, and made possible, the opportunity for her to grow into who she had become. Her love for them was unconditional, yet, they were never able to express their love in return — if indeed, any love for her ever really existed. Julie was also very taken with Ernie's insistence that he be with her to support her.

A few hours later, Julie and Ernie entered a waiting room at Georgetown University Hospital in D.C. After a few minutes wait, they were met by a doctor. She offered her condolences to Julie and explained that her grandmother, Jennifer Luce Winton, had passed.

"How long ago did she die?" Julie asked.

"It was about an hour ago," the doctor replied.

"About the time our plane set down at Ronald Reagan airport," Julie said.

"I'm so sorry you couldn't have been here with her," the doctor said.

"I am too," Julie returned. "I guess it was just her time. What can you tell me about my grandfather?"

"We can offer a little better news about the senator. He has actually rallied some — his ability to speak is almost back."

"May we see him?" Then she added, "I'm sorry doctor, this is my friend, Ernie Gravnick. He came with me from Chicago."

"Hello, Mr. Gravnick."

"Yes, Ms. Winton, I'll have a nurse take you to the senator's room. But, if Mr. Gravnick is not immediate family, he'll need to stay out here in the waiting room. Senator Winton's room is #8347, down here on the left." The nurse opened the door for her.

While Julie's eyes adjusted to the darkened room, she saw her grandfather sleeping.

Suddenly his eyes opened and he said softly, "I'm awake."

"Grandpa,"Julie said with a sigh. "I believe you're back with us."

His voice was hardly a whisper. "Julie? It's you!"

"Yes, it's me," she said. She laid her hand on his arm.

"Your hand feels so good — nice and warm. They keep it so cold in here. I'm freezing."

"I know," she said, "you poor dear. But when it's cold, germs can't spread."

"They kill the germs, and they knock off the patients same time."

Julie snickered at his joke. "Oh, Grandpa Harry."

He smiled. "I'm so glad you're here…"

"I am too, Grandpa," Julie answered, a soft smile on her lips. "Where else would I be at a time like this?"

"I have something to tell you."

"It's all right, you can tell me later."

"You need to know this now. It's something that should have been told to you long ago — and now, with Grandma gone, and not certain that I'll survive, I must tell you…"

Realizing that the Senator was aware that his wife had died, Julie decided to let him talk. "Okay, Grandpa. Tell me, I'm listening."

"It's something I could never say before — while Grandma was alive. I wanted to but we made a pact with each other when you were a baby — never to tell you. But, now you have a right to know."

"Know what Grandpa? Tell me. What could be so terrible, that you and Grandma have kept it secret all these years?"

"It's about your mother."

"I know about my mother. You told me that she died in an automobile accident along with my father. It happened while they were on the way to the hospital, where I was supposed to be born."

"Yes, that is what happened…and when the police and the paramedics got there, they found you alive. The accident caused you to be born."

"Yes, I know. But there's something else — isn't there?"

"I'm so sorry, so ashamed. What we never told you was…that your mother was Jewish."

"She was Jewish? That's it? So what!"

"But you see in the Jewish religion, the child of the mother is also considered Jewish."

"Yeah, I know that. So, if I'm Jewish…that also makes Jonathan Jewish. Right? I can't wait to tell Gravnick…His father was Jewish and though his mother, Dora, is Catholic, Ernie grew up in his Uncle Sol's house, and he considers himself a Jew. He doesn't follow all the rituals, he told me that his Aunt Sylvia always lit candles on Friday night,and they celebrated Shabbat. The Jewish Sabbath."

"Then you're not angry with Grandma Jennifer and me?"

"No, I'm not angry with you. But why on earth did you find it necessary to hide my mother's religion from me?"

He shook his head sadly. "You have every right to be angry with us. The fact is, we were ashamed. We never let your mother into our family. We wanted nothing to do with her."

"But why Grandfather?"

He shook his head again. "We were downright anti-Semetic. We never even met her. Didn't want to meet her. We even refused to let your father bring her around."

"But, you were good people — very special people — honored for all the many wonderful things you did. Why, were you so against my mother? What did she do?"

"She did nothing bad. Actually, she was a fashion designer. A pretty good one, from what we were told. They said, had she lived, she would have been very successful."

"How could you ever have been so bigoted?"

"I suppose you'll never truly understand. It's was the way we were raised. To be perfectly honest, growing up, I never knew anyone who was Jewish. The first Jew I ever met, was in the service…in boot camp. That man was excluded in every way imaginable. The other soldiers wanted nothing to do with him. Later on, I heard he'd been killed on Omaha Beach. The rumor was that he was hit by friendly fire."

"He was murdered? That's horrible. How could they…how could *you* be so uncaring? Did you report this?" Julie asked.

"No one reported it." For a while the old man was quiet.

Then, breathing deeply and rubbing his eyes, he said, "I know it was wrong. Back then, I never thought about it at all. Our friends, they were like we were. They believed Jews were different. That they weren't like other people. We stayed away from them…didn't associate with them. To be honest, we were afraid. Afraid, if anyone were to find out our son was married to a Jew, he would have been ostracized…more-so, *we* were concerned, that we too, would be socially excluded — ignored. Then, you came along and our concern increased. We were afraid you wouldn't be able to get into the schools *we* wanted for you…or be accepted into the right social circles."

"What you are telling me is that, you were taught to hate. You and all your bigoted friends were just like you. But tell me something — how come you never taught *me* to hate? I guess, I wasn't good enough even for that. Your own granddaughter. I was one of the hated, wasn't I? Is that why — no matter how hard I tried — or how good my grades were — or how successful I became — never, did you, or Grandmother — offer me a pat on the back. You never said, not even once, "Well done, kid." All because I was a Jew?"

"No, no." Her grandfather's voice was weak, trembling. "We really loved you. I love you. Maybe not so much at first. But very quickly, we learned to love and accept you as our own. I admit — right off, we did see you as being different. I don't know how much we realized it at the time — we probably ignored you more than we should have. We shuffled you off to a nanny whenever possible. We were hardly ever there for you. I can't remember if we stayed away on purpose or not…but, probably we weren't ready to accept the situation for what it really was. Then, having you around and seeing you grow, dissolved whatever bad feelings we had. We began to see you as a very special little girl. Both in and out of school. As you grew into a bright and talented teen, we, meaning Grandma and me, had numerous discussions — we realized that you had a right to know — to know everything about your mother — to know everything about yourself — to know you were a Jew, and if you so wished, to allow you the choice of following the Jewish faith."

"But you never told me. Why not?"

"We really wanted to, but each time we would make a decision to tell you, we backed off — we worried about how you would take it — would it upset you? Would you become angry and reject us? It was selfish of us, but we loved you so much, we couldn't take the chance of losing you."

"So, you did nothing."

"It's true. We did nothing. We let everything go on the way it was. We were afraid to upset the applecart. I know you won't understand, and I can't blame you if you don't believe it, but try as we might, we were just unable to tell you. Yet, deep down, we were so proud of you — of everything you did. We never missed an opportunity to tell our friends or anyone else we would run into. We bragged about you. If someone would listen, we'd tell them about all the exceptional things you were doing, or had done."

"But you never said anything to me."

"That was our misfortune. Not just yours."

Julie didn't know what to say. Tears filled her eyes.

"Can you ever forgive us? Even if you can't forgive me, now that Grandma is gone, can you at least forgive her?"

"You know what Grandpa? I *am* going to forgive you. Both you and Grandma. And do you know why I forgive you? It's because no one should ever have to carry around the kind of hate, the two of you have obviously been made to bear all these years. It needs to end — now. If I don't forgive you, the hate would continue to carry on with me — I'd probably end up shuffling that hate off to others around me — particularly to those close to me — to those I love the most, like my son Jonathan. Well, I won't do that. I refuse to do that."

"I'm going to let you in on something else. Something that should relieve a great deal of your guilt as well. Due to your selfish treatment of me, I truly believe it inadvertently, made me strive harder to be successful than I might have done otherwise. I wanted, no, I craved your love and attention so much that, that no matter how hard, or impossible things may have seemed at the time, I was just unable to give up. I had to prove to you that I could do it — and by trying to prove it to you, I proved it myself. So thank you Grandfather Harry. And yes, I love you too."

Chapter Forty

After the case against Julie Winton was dropped, the news of her release spread quickly. As usual, the newspaper editorials and so-called experts on TV, the contributors who try to help the news anchors seem like they know what they're talking about, were rampant. People who loved Julie, were much relieved — others said she got away with murder — she got off on a technicality.

Another, less followed story being floated and discussed in some circles, had to do with a new copy of hospital security tapes, in the hands of the Highland Park Police.

Both stories drew more than passing curiosity from Roy. She would drop her interest in Julie Winton, however, pending further notice, if any, from her client. Her attitude toward the security tapes no longer wetted her appetite. They were unimportant now. She would eliminate future use of the obese, Hispanic, hospital attendant from her repertoire. It could be a potential liability. However, the chubby fellow would be missed. Roy truly enjoyed playing the part. These were typical of the ups and downs in her profession. She took them in stride and rolled with the punches. That's what a professional does.

The casual, assured demeanor of Anthony Russo had been shaken by the hit and run death of his daughter Jennifer. That's what one would expect of a loving father. Indeed, Anthony did mourn for his daughter — for a day or two — right up until her killer, Junior Giaconte had been taken out. With the burden of revenge lifted, Russo filed the incident away under old business and set out to continue life as it was. But, what was, was not to continue.

Almost imperceptible at first, a strange face showed up at one of his places of business. Outsiders seldom frequented any of Russo's enterprises. An occasional unknown person asking questions was noticed and immediately reported to a supervisor, who in-turn notified Mr. Russo.

When Gravnick visited Russo at his home, he was the first outsider to breech his privacy of his new residence. Though not happy about it, Russo accepted the visit as protocol, all in the course of business. He didn't like having the Highland Park cops there because they'd seen where and how he lived. This was particularly upsetting as Gravnick knew of his previous residence on Kedzie Avenue, where he seemingly lived a quiet, modest life.

Russo was very much aware that in his business he should not let people see him living a luxurious lifestyle. Actually, he bought the house as an investment. As a high-end rental it would throw-off a good cash flow. However, before renting it out, he decided to see what it would be like living in such a place. It was intended to be for a short time. Perhaps, a week or two at most. Like taking a vacation. But, he found it so much more enjoyable than being in the city at the old house. He rationalized that no one need know where he really lived. He'd keep the old place, but enjoy the quiet life of the suburbs most of the time.

Gravnick had also annoyed him with some of the questions he asked, but Russo let them go by as well, because he was investigating Jennifer's death. What had happened the last couple of weeks however, was much more disconcerting. A so-called city worker showed up at his commercial laundry business, supposedly checking on their business license — then someone from the utility company happened by one of his restaurant's — another day it was a college student, working on a *bullshit* school project at one of his construction sites. Hearing of these incidents, he knew they were matters to be handled.

A meeting was held with the head of each of Russo's business entities. They were given a heads up to be even more on guard in the future; not only to report any visits by outsiders — be sure to pay specific attention to any and all questions a visitor may ask — write them down — if possible record them. He needed to know if there was pattern to their questions.

CHAPTER FORTY-ONE

Sir Harry survived his stroke — so did his ability to speak — he regained enough feeling and motion in his right arm and hand to feed himself. After a period in rehab, Julie made arrangements to have him flown to Chicago where he was then transported to the Deerfield Nursing Home.

The knighted, ex-senator, retired two-star general, international hero, had never encountered anyone like Dora Gravnick. He thought he had seen and heard it all. The words that came from her mouth mostly embarrassed him. They also startled, amazed, and intrigued him. She never minced words — said what was on her mind — straight forward and direct. She was a force to be reckoned with. He said she was his punishment for all the bad things he had ever done. He told Julie not to tell Dora, but in spite of her wicked tongue, he liked her. She would be a challenge for him in his waning days.

With a new understanding of herself, of who she really was, Julie set out to continue life to the fullest. When she told Gravnick about her Jewish heritage, he took it as she knew he would.

"So, you'll have to learn how to make chicken soup —Jewish penicillin. Oh, Dora will give you her recipe for matzo balls. And by the way, I like my gefilte fish made with Lake Superior white fish. Most of all, you must get Aunt Sylvia's recipe for chopped liver — it's the best. She adds saltines. The crackers make it real light."

"What's with you? I find out I'm Jewish and all you do is talk about food."

"Well, that's what Jewish people talk about. They finish breakfast and ask, "What's for lunch?" After lunch it's, "What's for dinner?" That's how it goes. It's meant to be. In Yiddish they'd say, "It's *b'shairt*. It's meant to be.""

Julie mimicked. "It's *b'shairt*. I like that…*b'shairt*. It's meant to be."

"Seriously, have you given any thought about a Jewish education, either for yourself, or Jonathan?"

"I have never been that much of a traditional believer. When I was young, my grandparents took me to church. But, once I got in high school, I kind of lost interest. At this point, I don't know. I'll need to think about it — mainly for Jonathan — if he shows any interest. I'll discuss it with him."

Julie was determined that whatever her life would be in the future, it would include Jonathan and Gravnick. Ernie had already signed an agreement to become Jonathan's guardian in the event anything happened to her. He did this when she went to jail. All she had to do was get him to marry her. She knew he loved her — and he and Jonathan were a thing. But, with all that happened they'd never broached the subject of marriage. Being that Gravnick was kind of old fashioned, she preferred he'd ask her. But if he didn't, she knew she would.

Meanwhile, life continued. Between her detainment in jail, having to go to D.C., settling her grandmother's affairs and getting her grandfather resettled, several weeks had gone by. She knew that Jenn Wooten had everything under control, but the business really needed her. Or, perhaps it was that she just wanted to get back to work? She called Jenn to let her know that she was back in town and would be coming in the next day.

Jenn informed her that she had some candidates lined up for her or Ernie to interview for the job openings at the house. She also told her that the contractor had called to inform them that the work at Belle Vista would be completed next week.

Gravnick too, had to play catch-up. The little fishing trip the department had planned for the Ghost never got a bite. Sampson was disappointed. "I really thought the Ghost would have been lured by our bait. I guess I was wrong."

Gravnick said, he wasn't sure. "Maybe the news of Paul Diamond's suicide and the dismissal of Julie's case made him wary. Or it could have been because the Ghost's efforts to get Julie sent to jail didn't work so, he just backed off."

In a meeting with Jack Dilly and Sampson, Gravnick was brought up to date on their undercover surveillance of Anthony Russo. This included in-person visits to a few of the man's business sites. In each situation they had witnessed nothing unusual. "It's going to be tough to come up with any hard evidence on him. Mr. Russo covered his tracks well," said Dilly.

"How many actual contacts were been made with Russo's people?" Gravnick asked.

"Our people completed just three one-on-one contacts," said Dilly.

"Okay. Continue the surveillance, but let's hold up on any more contact with his people. I don't want them to get suspicious of us watching them. Besides, we don't know what the Chicago cops have been doing. They've possibly made their own contacts. I'll call Charley House. If they've done as we have, chances are Russo's already got his eyes and ears up."

The next day Julie was in her office by 7 a.m. She plowed through her mail and correspondence, returned phone calls, met with department heads and in a crescendo of executive orders, brought the morning to a finale at a working lunch with Jenn Wooten.

After she finished up with Jenn, Julie spent the next couple of hours interviewing prospects to replace Dylan Sullivan as her chauffeur and body guard, and to fill other household positions at Belle Vista.

Toward the middle of that afternoon, Gravnick received a call form Julie. She told him she had a couple of prospects coming by for the jobs at the house. She wanted him to meet them before she hired them. Asked if eight o'clock that evening would be good for him, Ernie said he'd be there.

The doorbell rang precisely at eight. Gravnick said, "Right on time. That's a gold star for their side." Opening the door, he was surprised to see two women. One looked to be in her late forties or early fifties, medium height and well rounded. Not fat, but of solid build. The other was all woman, tall, perhaps 5'9"— every angle and curve, precisely where it should have been. Her age was deceptive. She could have been in her thirties or forties. He could not tell. Ernie introduced himself and bid them in.

The shorter woman spoke with a distinct British accent, stated her name as Darby Den. She let it be known that it was Mrs. Den, and may be addressed as such. The other woman introduced herself as Telli Wonder. He led them from the foyer to the living room where Julie awaited them. As Telli moved across the room, Ernie noted that the bounce and jiggle of her body parts defined her name. She was indeed a wonder.

By the time Gravnick read the resumes of the two candidates and he and Julie had asked all pertinent questions, Ernie learned that Darby Den, had been married to a greatly admired high school principal, who had recently been run down by a drugged-out, underage driver. Prior to her marriage, she worked as housekeeper and cook to a British Lord and his family for fifteen years. While in that position, she was charged with the care of a ten bedroom Estate, did the food shopping for the family and supervised three others servants, including two maids and a gardener. She and her husband had been married barely two years. "Due to his death I was forced to give up our lovely home in Wilmette, Illinois — the only place I'd known since coming to this country. As you can see, I'm not looking for just a job, but a family to care for."

Telli Wonder told a whole different story. She was an ex-secret service agent, turned professional wrestler, who was now looking for something a little less strenuous. "I believe I have the perfect skills to protect Ms. Winton and her family. As your chauffeur, I can offer the added ability of being trained as a competitive driver. Which, from what I understand, may have been helpful in a recent incident you encountered in front of your home.

Julie and Ernie were impressed by what they had heard and seen. Both women seemed perfect. They answered every question directly…even asked a few of their own. Jenn had done a thorough pre-check of their references and each had gotten rave reviews. Jenn's questioning of Lord Henley, Darby Den's old employer in Oxford, was enlightening. He stated, "To be completely honest, I would have to say that Mrs. Den had but one flaw. She is very direct — knew what she wanted — insisted one call her "Mrs. Den."

Julie and Gravnick agreed. They shook hands with Telli Wonder and Darby Den — the two would take up their new positions a week from Monday — moving day at Belle Vista. They would reside in the two newly-built suites above the six car garage.

CHAPTER FORTY-TWO

"When police Captain Charley House picked up his phone, he heard the familiar greeting of his friend Ernie Gravnick. "Good morning, Charley Horse. How's everything hanging?"

"Gravnick — you're back in town. Sorry to hear about Julie's grandmother. How's Julie taking it?"

"She's okay. Thanks for asking, Charley. Tell me where the Chicago police are on Russo."

"We've been observing — rotating our stake-outs, so as to not to draw attention.

One of our officers paid a visit to a suspected laundry facility. Posed as a representative of a large exterminating company considering a change in laundries to handle their uniforms. They discussed the quality of their work and potential pricing. She reported everything seemed in order. Noticed nothing unusual."

"We too have run a series of operations — observed who and what went in and came out. My people made direct contacts with three of Russo's business operations. Like your officers, they too, came up empty. For the time being we've continued our stake-outs, but have deferred any further direct contacts. We don't want to spook them."

Charley agreed with Gravnick. "Let's hope they're not already onto us."

"My thoughts exactly...we'll see. Stay in touch."

—◦◦—

Anthony Russo made periodic drive-by observations of his own business establishments. It wasn't because he didn't trust his employees or what they told him. Of course he didn't trust them. They were all crooks. The reason for the drive-by appearances was to satisfy his own distrust of humanity. Russo didn't get to be where he was by trusting people. He got there because of the one person he could trust — himself. He always checked and double checked. For the purpose of these little excursions, which he dubbed "sightseeing tours," he drove a not too old, yet not too new, not too dirty, not too clean, grayish, four door, mid-size, any-brand sedan. He could drive this car most anywhere in the city and be, if not invisible, most certainly unnoticeable.

On his last tour in the phantom car, Anthony proved his paranoia was not for naught. He always saw what others missed. The telephone company truck parked down the street from his wholesale fish market, was not what it seemed. His drive-by unveiled someone inside, staring down the action that emerged from a delivery truck in front of the market — one of his men paying off the driver for whatever he had delivered. Though the person doing the staring couldn't see the white plastic bags hidden among the shipment of slimy seafood, the telescope held to his eye was certainly an attempt to get an intimate close-up of the action at hand. Russo's hunch was right. When his managers mentioned strangers stopping by, asking questions, he knew something was going on.

Seeing the telephone truck staked-out, was proof the cops have been sniffing around. But sniffing meant nothing. If they smelled anything, they'd have raided the place and shut it down. Russo's people would continue operating in the normal course of business. They'd keep their antennae up — always on the alert. Russo would make one small change. The where and the how of their distribution system would be revised. Should the cops think they saw something and decide to pay a visit with a subpoena, they'd find nothing but smelly fish. That's what happened when you stir up the waters before you drop your bait.

But, one unanswered question remained — who was doing the sniffing? The locals or the Feds? Russo needed to find out.

—◦◦—

A few days later Julie, Jonathan and Gravnick were at Belle Vista waiting for the arrival of the moving truck. It was moving day. Darby Den and Telli Wonder, were in the kitchen busily washing down the cabinets and lining the shelves. Though Telli was not expected to do housework, she willingly offered to help out. Mrs. Den objected strenuously. This was her domain. Her work. It was what she was hired to do. She was in charge of the house. Telli diplomatically explained she was aware of Mrs. Den's domain and had no desire to interfere with or usurp her authority. She was there, waiting around for the movers and just wanted to help. Mrs. Den, relented.

Julie and Gravnick were delighted that the two women seemed to get on well together.

They'd made a good choice in hiring them. By the end of the day, the movers had been there. Everything had been put in place, including Jonathan's dark room with all of his equipment and cameras. Belle Vista was restored to what it had been. It was indeed a magnificent house. More than that, it was home.

The next morning began with Mrs. Den serving up a breakfast of her own recipe sour cream pancakes, assorted berries, chicken sausages and coffee, tea or milk. After breakfast, Jonathan and Ernie got up ready to clear the table, when Mrs. Den rushed in to tell them "No, no. Leave the dishes. I'll clear up." Meanwhile, Telli had brought the limo around to the driveway and was waiting to take Julie to her office. Jonathan left with Gravnick. Ernie, would drop him off at school on his way to the station. Mrs. Den and Telli Wonder, were off to a splendid start.

Several weeks passed. Life at last seemed back to normal. Winton Cosmetics Industries was having a banner year. Julie's TV series, *The Beautiful You*, was nominated for an Emmy as Best Reality Show of the year. Julie was back at the helm and fully involved. Moreover, she was looking for new ways to grow the company, both from within and through acquisition.

The Highland Park Police Department had also settled into a more normal, certainly less hectic operation. Ernie Gravnick was officially installed as Chief of Police of that Chicago suburb. For the time being he decided not to replace himself as Chief of Detectives. He could handle both roles. It had been that way for some time. After all, nothing had really changed.

That included the circumstances of all the department's open cases. None of them had been solved. Not Winton/Wilder, the attempted hit and run in Geneva, the bombing in Zurich or the attack on Gravnick. Not the fire-bombing at Belle Vista, the murder of Giaconte, Junior, the attempted frame-up of Julie Winton, or the burning of hospital tapes at the Highland Park Station. In the end, only God knew where their suspicions of Russo might lead.

Though Gravnick always carried the weight of uncertainty from his father's and grandfather's deaths, his life with his adopted family went beyond his expectations. He could hardly believe that what had started as a disastrous situation had turned into his living with one of the most beautiful women in the world, in her home, that to him was like a castle. To top it off, he now had a surprising fondness for her son, who when he first met him was an eccentric introvert.

That night, they sat at the dinner table, enjoying Mrs. Den's wonderful fare — Provencal veal stew with club sauce followed by her own unique bananas foster. Julie smiled and said, "Isn't this wonderful — the three of us together? Are the two of you as happy as I am?"

Ernie patted his stomach and replied, "I can't think of anything better." Jonathan's response caught them both off guard. "Ernie, why don't you and Mom get married, so we could be a real family — and I'd have a real dad?"

"Jonathan, I don't think there's anything in this world I'd like more than that. But I don't know if your mom would marry me. Furthermore, I'm just a common cop. Your mom could certainly do much better, I think."

Gravnick looked directly at Julie, "Would you really marry a chump like me?"

Julie looked back at him, her face reflecting deep thought. She shrugged her shoulders. "I don't know." She brought her hand to her face, resting her chin on it. "This is so sudden. Could you give me some time to think it over?"

Gravnick nodded. But his face was crest-fallen.

Julie continued. "I'm going to need at least month or two. After all, this is a major decision, and as you just said, you are a bit of a chump."

Then she started laughing.

Gravnick looked puzzled.

"Of course I'll marry you, you wonderful idiot. I've been waiting for you to ask me. You know I love you. Come here and kiss me before I change my mind." Gravnick got up from the table and he and Julie hugged.

Jonathan watched, softly laughing.

The following weeks progressed with the announcement of their upcoming marriage. Ernie, proudly told everyone he was going to be a father. He would officially adopt Jonathan. Everyone was happy for them. Especially Dora Gravnick. When Julie and Ernie told her they would marry, she got so excited, she yelled "Holy Shit!" at the top of her lungs.

CHAPTER FORTY-THREE

Anthony Russo's attention to detail paid off. It was not long after he spotted the stake-out at his wholesale fish market, that the police made a full scale raid on the place. They found nothing but slimy, smelly fish, as he predicted. He also, noted that the warrant was signed by a municipal judge and the cops were locals. This was good. It meant that the authorities were just guessing. If they had real evidence, the Feds would have been all over it.

The city cops were a lot less suspicious, but just to make sure they were on the job, he mentioned to various people he knew to keep a wary eye on anything that seemed out of the ordinary.

⸻

It had been a long steady rise to the top for Anthony Russo. Relaxing in the privacy of his personal spa at the mansion on Cody Drive, he reminisced on how it all began. He remembered the day his boyhood friend, Sal Giaconte, Sr. introduced him to Don Franko Pistale.

How the years go by, he thought, as he reviewed his early life. How it all happened …

In a moment, a flash, he was back in the famous old restaurant. He was a kid again.

There was the Don seated at his special table in the back of the Ristorante

Italiano. He knew from stories that Sal had told him, that the Don was the king of Chicago's South Side syndicate. Sal, who was a couple of years older than Russo, had begun working for Pistale shortly after dropping out of high school.

Giaconte had been like a big brother to Anthony from the time he started school. Back then Anthony's family name was Roccolo. He was born, Anthony Roccolo. The Giacontes were neighbors of the Roccolo's and Tony's mother had asked the older boy to walk him the three blocks to the elementary school each day. She paid Sal two dollars a week for seeing that he got to school and returned home safely.

Though younger, Tony was exceptionally smart, especially in math. Because of the kid, Sal's math grades soon began to improve. After that, Giaconte decided to keep Tony close by. In spite of their age difference, they became pals. More than that, they were like brothers — always together. They became known as "The Inseparables." Sal Giaconte and Tony Roccolo — all through school, they were like one.

When he introduced Tony to Don Franko Pistale, Giaconte said, "This here's my friend, Tony Roccolo. I told you about him. He's the one that graduated from high school. He's a math genius."

Franko Pistale raised his napkin to his lips, wiped them once, and said to Tony Roccolo, "You're afraid of me, aren't you?"

Tony smiled. "Should I be?"

The Don turned to Giaconte and said, "I like this kid. He's got guts." He then moved over, patted the seat with his hand "Sit down young man. Have something to eat. The food's good here."

He yelled to the waiter standing nearby, "Hey, bring the kid a menu." Then, turning back to Tony he said, "You want a job, kid?"

The following day he was running numbers for Don Franko Pistale.

Two years later, the Don put Roccolo in charge of his numbers business. Roccolo also found himself advising Pistale on anything to do with logistics or money. He was becoming a trusted consigliere.

Tony's steady rise within the ranks of Don Franko's organization had not been missed by Roccolo's friend Sal Giaconte. Sal didn't like it one bit that Tony was edging up on him. Giaconte was the Don's man. A while back, Pistale had even given him a small piece of the take. It's true, Giaconte wanted more. But he was patient. His time would come. He'd bide his time and wait for the right moment. Then he'd take it all from the old man. However, Pistale's increased dependency on Roccolo was making Sal feel insecure. Giaconte didn't like the feeling at all. He began to think that the time to make his move on Don Franko was drawing near. Then, in the privacy of the Don's office, Pistale gave him the surprise of his life.

Suddenly, Tony was in Pistale's office discussing various matters with him. At the conclusion of their business, the Don said, "I need you to hang around a few minutes." He got up, walked to the closed office door, opened it and bellowed, "Giaconte, get your ass in here. Now."

With the two men seated opposite him, Don Franko Pistale laid out his plan. He told them that it was his intention to take over Don Caesar Casilone's Westside organization. Casalone's operation was double the size of Pistale's, but that was what he needed. The overall take of his operation had begun to slide. This was in spite of a substantial increase in Roccolo's numbers business. But the organization's other operations had all seen a downturn — and weren't about to improve. There was just less money available now and the way to turn it around was to combine Casalone's business with his. There had been some discussions between the two men about a possible merger, but Casalone showed little interest. Pistale's decision was made. Take Casalone out and then own his territory.

Pistale's orders were for Giaconte to have Caesar Casilone followed day and night until the right situation arose. The Don would have his men ready for whenever Giaconte gave the go ahead.

—⟡—

The time finally came when one of Giaconte's spies, a maid at Dora and Jesse Gravnick's house, overheard Ernie Gravnick telling his mother and father that Poppee would take him to the Brookfield Zoo on Saturday.

When the meeting in Don Franko's office broke up and Giaconte and Tony headed for the door, Pistale called Roccolo back. He had something more he wanted to say to him. Taking Tony into his confidence he said, "I want you to stay close to Giaconte until this thing is done. Salvatore does good work, but he's a little too ambitious. Given the opportunity, I have no doubt he'd try to take me out. I've given him a small interest in the organization that has so far, kept him in place. With this new venture, I don't want him getting any ideas of grandeur. Keep an eye on him, understand?"

Following the successful hit on Casalone at the Brookfield Zoo, which became known as the *Grand Massacre at Brookfield*, Don Franko assigned his most
loyal people to take over the Westside operation. He also praised Giaconte for a
job well done, then told him in no uncertain terms, "Salvatore — you should be
a dead man."

Giaconte looked on in disbelief.

Pistale continued, "You need to know that I am aware of what's been
going on in that traitorous head of yours. You should also know that if you ever
try to take me out, or think about taking over my organization, the whole world
will know that the perpetrator of the *Grand Massacre at Brookfield* was you.
Furthermore, my friend the SA will see that all the boys that were with you, will
be witnesses against you. So, from here on, you will be a good boy and do exactly as I say. Understood?"

Giaconte nodded, and said, "Yes, sir."

"You're wondering what I'm going to do with you next, aren't you?"

"Yes, sir."

"Well, Salvatore Giaconte, I am going to put you in a place where you
will be watched every minute of your day by people who are most loyal to me.
They will immediately tell me if you so much as fart wrong. Do you also understand that, Sal?"

"Yes, Don Pistale. I understand."

"Since I know you will never forget where you stand, you will continue to
work for me."

"Thank you. Thank you, Don Pistale."

"You will even keep the percentage of the take I previously gave you."

"I don't deserve such generosity, Don Pistale."

"That's right, you don't. But, nice guy that I am, not only do you get to
keep the original percentage, but I'm going to double the amount of your take."

"Thank you, sir."

"You don't need to thank me, Giaconte. The reason I'm doing this is that
you're going to run the Westside organization for me...and by having a reasonable stake in the business you're going to work your ass off knowing that the
more I make, the more you'll make."

Giaconte was dumb-struck. "You mean I'll be Don of the Westside?"

"Not quite. You can call yourself anything you want, but you're still working for me. You will merely manage the business — for me. I am the only Don
around here. I'm the one that gives the orders. The boys that surround you will

take their orders from me. As I said, you can call yourself anything you damn well please, Don, shmon — I care not what the outside world thinks — only that you know who you work for — and should you ever cross me — you're dead."

Over the years that followed, one man survived, that knew the truth of who took over the Westside mob and who gave the ultimate order for the hit on Don Caesar Casilone — the hit that also killed Jesse Gravnick. The man was Tony Roccolo. He had become like a son to Don Pistale — and the eventual heir to the throne.

CHAPTER FORTY-FOUR

By the time Roccolo took over from Franko Pistale, the business had changed — the real money was in illegal drugs. More money than he previously thought possible. Being a shrewd businessman, Roccolo decided to take the operation underground. He rejected the title of "Don." He also changed his name. Tony Roccolo ceased to exist. He replaced himself with Anthony Russo and lived a low-profile, middle class life.

Anthony married and had a family — a daughter they named Jennifer. When Jennifer was two years old, Russo's wife was diagnosed with an incurable disease. She died three weeks later. From then on, it was the loving father and his daughter, who Anthony truly adored.

Russo, quietly bought up business after business. As he threw off the yoke of the old time mob, Anthony became totally involved with moving drugs. He rebuilt the whole organization and operated it his way. The business grew quickly and Russo began to look for larger, even more successful companies to acquire. He needed them to move the overwhelming amount of cash that was coming through from the sale of drugs.

Before anyone knew what happened, he had become the largest distributor of illegal drugs in the Chicago metro. That would grow to encompass the entire state of Illinois — and within the next few years, Russo controlled drug distribution in all states east of the Mississippi.

About that time, while eating at his Club in Highland Park, he was introduced to well-known advertising executive, Thornton Burnet Wilder. He had heard of Wilder and knew he was married to Julie Winton, the billionaire founder and CEO of Winton Cosmetics, International. With the growth of his organization and his cash hoards needing to be washed, Russo thought to himself, *"If I controlled a company like that I could bury a hell of a lot of cash."*

The two men seemed to get along and at Russo's suggestion, they would meet in town for lunch quite regularly. With carefully placed hints, Russo began to ferret Wilder out, asking him questions about Winton Cosmetics stock. He knew the company was listed on the NYSE. He asked Wilder how many shares of the company Julie owned.

"Does she ever worry about someone buying up too many shares — launching an hostile takeover bid for the company?" Russo asked.

Russo had guessed right about Thornton. His question had found a weak spot regarding Thornton's wife. Was he jealous of her wealth and prestige? It turned out he was more than a little jealous of Julie. In fact, Thornton was extremely envious of her position. He actually came up with a carefully contrived plan to buy up Winton Cosmetics stock without bringing it to the attention of the Security and Exchange Commission.

Anthony was very impressed by Wilder's plan and over the next several months, their people had bought up enough shares to grant them control of Winton Cosmetics.

Wilder then told Russo that since the plan was his idea, he wanted a bigger piece of the action. This was a big mistake. Thornton misjudged the man he was dealing with — Russo didn't need Wilder.

However, the thugs he hired to do the hit bungled the job. Taking out Wilder was no problem. But Julie was another story.

The thugs underestimated how hard this woman could fight back. In the ensuing fight, they did some real damage to her head. They left her barely alive. "The boss ain't going to like this," one mumbled to the other as they left the apartment.

With the murder of Wilder and Julie Winton in the hospital with critical injuries, Russo knew he had to lay low. Any semblance of a takeover of Winton Cosmetics at the time, would immediately be suspect. He'd have to wait. No one knew how long Julie might remain in a coma — if she'd ever come out of it — if she'd survive her injuries — and if she survived, what condition she might be in.

Julie not only survived, she made a miraculous recovery and eventually resumed her position at Winton Cosmetics and was welcomed back on her TV show with a gala broadcast which included cast, live audience and celebrity guests.

Anthony Russo knew the timing was still not right to try for a takeover of Julie's company. There was too much going on. The police hadn't gotten anywhere in their search for the murderer of Thornton B. Wilder or the attempted murder of Julie Winton. But he knew the reputation of the Highland Park's Police Chief, Ernie Gravnick — had actually met him several years back. Gravnick was then a police detective in Chicago and Russo's name had come up in connection with a case he was investigating. Gravnick was not someone to fool with. He knew the man wouldn't give up. Russo just might need to take him out, or in the least, scare him off.

When Russo got word from his contacts in Europe, that Gravnick had been making inquiries through Interpol, concerning unusually large amounts of cash being moved around, he knew for certain, he had to keep an eye on him. In order to set up the purchases of Winton stock, he had wired funds in and out of multiple banks around the world — many of them in EU countries. Just in case, Russo would be prepared.

Though he knew about a mysterious hitman with a reputation for absolutely clean kills, he had never used him. The man's charges were outrageous and he demanded 100% payment up front. Some called him the Ghost. Those who had used him claimed, he was worth every penny. Russo would find out. He sent out a call and put the Ghost on standby.

The day Gravnick left for Zurich, a beautiful brunette boarded the same flight — took the seat immediately behind him. Her prime mission was to watch him and scare him off, if necessary. In the event that didn't work, he was ordered to use force of another kind.

"Kill him, only as a last resort," his client said.

Roy found Gravnick to be tougher than he'd expected. He employed all of his wily skills, but still the cop got away with his life. When Gravnick was brought back to the States, the Ghost was instructed to lay low. When Gravnick recuperated and returned to work, she received further instructions.

While busy gobbling up the underworld of drugs, Anthony somehow managed to be a devoted father to his beautiful and talented daughter, Jennifer Russo. He saw to it that she grew up in the lap of luxury until she was killed in her mid-twenties. Run down by Salvatore Giaconte, Junior — the son of his boyhood and lifelong friend.

—◝◟◞—

After being notified of the hit-and-run death of Jennifer, Anthony Russo swore to revenge her death. But this time there could be no mistakes made, as in the Winton/Wilder situation.

Once it turned out that Salvatore Giaconte, Junior was the suspect, Russo told the Ghost to "Kill the son of a bitch."

CHAPTER FORTY-FIVE

Julie had been giving her newly found Judaism a lot of thought. She discussed the situation with Jonathan — asked if he thought he would like to learn about Jewish history, study Torah — possibly become bar mitzvah? Jonathan knew that his mother and for that matter, his father, never went to church. When he was younger and saw that many of his friends attended church services with their parents, he asked his mother how come they didn't go to church. Julie told him, "As a child, my grandmother and grandfather belonged to the Presbyterian Church, and when they were home they'd take me with them to services. But as they weren't around all that much I guess it just didn't seem that important to me."

"To be honest, Mom, as you well know, religion has never been a part of my life. Out of curiosity, I have read some about why people are drawn to religious worship. I understand the concept of moral teachings that religions espouse. At most, my curiosity might lead me to read a book or two on Jewish history. I know they follow the Old Testament and we learned about the Holocaust in school. Otherwise, I'm a believer in facts. What I can see and what I can sense. I'm a science guy. There may be a higher power out there somewhere, but so far as I know there is no scientific proof."

The discussion with Jonathan left Julie thinking, that because of her casual outlook on religion and spirituality, she had deprived Jonathan of making an informed decision for himself. If for no other reason but to set an example for

Jonathan, she decided to talk to a Rabbi and find out what it would take for her to become reasonably educated in Judaism.

—⊙⌐~

It was a beautiful, cloudless Monday morning in September. Anthony Russo had scheduled the day for one of his sightseeing tours. As he drove casually by the building that housed his commercial laundry company, his attention was drawn to a group of dark-suited men who simultaneously stepped from the two SUVs parked directly in front. Each man carried the exact tan briefcase as they entered the main entrance, and were swallowed up inside the building.

Russo had driven but another block beyond the building when his phone rang. It was his business manager. He informed him that IRS auditors were there with a court order for an audit of the company's books. "What should I do, Boss?"

"What do you think you should do?" Russo asked. "Show them where the files are and be cooperative. That's what you do." Russo, knew the books they'd be looking at were clean. The real books were safely tucked away in his vault at home. Just the same, as his thumb clicked off the phone, Russo screamed out loud, "Fucking Feds. Who dragged them into this? They never knew I was even here. Damn. I should have known. It had to be Gravnick. The snooping all began after he showed up at the house. Before that, nobody ever bothered us. He's got to be the impetus behind this. It's a shame too. I kind of liked the man. He's a go-getter like me. But it's time for you to go, Chief Gravnick."

—⊙⌐~

By the time the wedding day approached, like everything else she'd ever done, Julie had immersed herself in religious studies — had gone so far as taking a class in Torah reading. She also decided that she wanted a Rabbi to marry them. Finding a Rabbi to perform the ceremony however, was not an easy task. Though Gravnick grew up in a Jewish home with his Uncle Sol and Aunt Sylvia, where they celebrated the Shabbat and Jewish holidays like Rosh Hashanah and Yom Kippur, and though his father was Jewish, his mother was not. Dora was Catholic. Under strict Jewish law, Gravnick was not considered Jewish. Nevertheless, she found a Reform Rabbi that agreed to marry them.

—⊙⌐~

Sampson, who had never stopped digging into Russo's past, ran into a wall when he could find nothing about the man prior to 1990. He looked at city and state records and found no birth certificate for Anthony Russo. 1990 was the first year a driver's license had been issued to him. Had he come from another state? The FBI checked if he had ever filled an income tax return prior to 1990. Nothing had been filled. Cross-referencing his social security number showed that one Tony Riccolo had filled annual tax returns with the identical social security number for several years prior to that time. With that information it took little time for them to find records indicating Tony Riccolo had officially changed his name to Anthony Russo in late 1989.

When Sampson showed the FBI report to Gravnick, he told him to keep on digging. "We need to know where Tony Riccolo worked and who he worked for. He was for the moment an unknown entity. "Get me something to hang on Tony Riccolo aka Anthony Russo. Great work, Sampson, keep on going with it."

Because of Gravnick's wish to adopt Jonathan and their desire to announce the adoption to everyone at the formal wedding, Julie and Ernie decided to have a judge marry them prior to the formal wedding. They completed all the adoption paperwork. This was done at Chicago City Hall with Jonathan and Sampson in attendance.

It was a magnificent day. The sun shone brightly over the green expanse of Ravinia Festival. A few puffy clouds floated in an otherwise clear periwinkle sky. This romantic venue, home to the oldest open air music park in the United States was further adorned that day, by flourishes of multicolored flowers that appeared to dance playfully wherever one's eyes wandered. Soft music accompanied the guests as they arrived.

Julie and Ernie talked about having a small, intimate wedding. Julie had not included the usual glut of industry and political acquaintances, inviting only family, family friends, and to quote Julie, "a few of my very close celebrity friends." Still, three hundred and fifty invitees wandered in to take their seats among the rows of chairs set up for the occasion.

Two very special guests seated in wheel chairs, chatted animatedly in the back. Dora Gravnick and retired senator, Sir Harry Winton attended the affair, having been brought there in a special limousine accompanied by Telli Wonder, the chauffeur, Mrs. Den and Sampson.

A small podium had been set in front of the grand stage that through the years has hosted the finest classical orchestras and soloists from around the world, as well as top contemporary music stars of today and yesteryear. Covering most of the podium was a Chuppah, the traditional Jewish wedding canopy, neatly draped across and held in place by posts on four corners.

The music changed, as Gravnick, accompanied by his best man, Charley House, entered from the right side and approached the podium. Gravnick smiled and nodded his head in recognition of a guest. The two men stood together on the right under the Chuppah. Everyone's attention was then drawn to the back of the aisle as the Matron of Honor made her entrance — Dora Gravnick, exhibiting the widest, brightest smile, was wheeled in her chair, by Jonathan, who slowly pushed her down the aisle and up a ramp to the podium. The two of them settled in opposite Ernie and Charley House.

A hush fell over the entire area as the music segued to the familiar opening chords of "The Wedding March." From the back center aisle, dressed in an overflowing gown of soft pink lace and satin, Julie Winton looked magnificent as she walked down the aisle, a smile on her face, accompanied by Sir Harry Winton. Her grandfather was given the honor of giving the bride away. He was gently wheeled in his chair by Sampson Bielegowski. Julie held onto her grandfather's arm until the halfway mark, where she eased her hand down to his unmoving fingers, brought his hand to her lips and kissed it lovingly. She then joined Ernie, who had stepped from the podium to meet his bride. He escorted her the remaining way to their place beneath the Chuppah. Sampson took Sir Harry to a space saved for him in the audience.

The music slowly faded to silence. A cough from a guest was heard. A chair moved.

The ceremony began with the Rabbi explaining that "We stand here beneath a Chuppah that signifies the home that you Ernie and Julie, will build together, as a couple. As you take your vows today, you take on the responsibility of not just loving each other, but caring for each other: For his needs and her needs. For his cares and her cares. For his wants and her wants. Being joined in matrimony is more than a legality or a religious ceremony, it is the merging of two souls into one. A successful marriage is not a situation in which two partners merely live together. Rather it is where each of you strive to know what the other is thinking, feeling and caring, almost without need for words. Each of you becomes as if one, yet you maintain your individuality."

Ernie was the first to read his vows. He told of his adoption of Jonathan and how excited he was to accept the responsibility of being a father to him, and soulmate to Julie. In turn, Julie promised to share herself, her life and her world, so long as they may live. They shared in an exchange of rings. They sipped the traditional wine, each from the same glass. The Rabbi pronounced them man and wife and told Ernie he may kiss his bride. While the two of them happily embraced, the Rabbi took the wine glass, wrapped it in a towel, and set it on the ground. As Gravnick raised his foot to complete the traditional breaking of the glass, Julie, suddenly cried, "No." Without further thought, she flung her body hard against Ernie, pushing him aside. The last thing Julie Winton-Gravnick saw before the bullet entered her brain was Telli Wonder, off to the side, aiming a telescopic rifle directly at Gravnick.

CHAPTER FORTY-SIX

In the chaos that followed the stomach-turning, hollow sound of the shot, people screamed. Many took cover under their seats. Others fell on top of their loved ones, seeking to protect them. Some just ran from the calamity of it all. Telli Wonder, alias Roy, aka as the Ghost or Spook, disappeared into a thick thatch of bushes directly behind where she had stood when she fired the shot. By the time anyone began a search, she had reappeared on other side of the park, as a yellow-haired, young man with a crew cut. But, she had made the first mistake of her career. She had hit the wrong target.

Devastated by Julie's death — by the realization that she had purposely taken a bullet meant for him, Gravnick, felt like a hollow core with nothing left inside. *How could she be gone?* He asked himself. *She had become my world. My life. My love. We had so many plans. Shit. Shit. Shit.*

Then he remembered, it was not just him anymore. He had a son. He had Jonathan. He was a dad. A dad with a responsibility to get him through this disaster. To nurture him. To help him grow and enjoy a meaningful life. He also had to find the son-of-a-bitch responsible for killing Julie. "If it takes the rest of my life — I'll get him my love."

It took but a few short weeks, with the unusual cooperation of the courts, local, state and federal law enforcement agencies, all working together, to turn Anthony Russo's life to misery. It should also be mentioned that working day and night, Sampson had meanwhile unraveled the life and mask from Anthony Russo, stripping him down to who he really was — Tony Riccolo, boyhood and lifelong friend of Salvatore Giaconte, Made Man and Consigliore to Don Franko Pistale, probable inheritor of, and present day king pin of Pistale's organized crime family. With this information, daily raids by the authorities that were conducted at most anytime of the day or night, encompassed the entirety of Russo's holdings including the mansion in Highland Park and his old house on W. Kedzie Avenue, where they also found and confiscated, millions of shares of Winton Cosmetics, International, Inc stock.

In the end when the judge's gavel came down, though he remained a suspect in the killing of Thornton Burnett Wilder, they were unable to convict Russo for murder. What was proven against Anthony Russo were several counts of drug distribution and money laundering, income tax evasion, operating a massage parlor without a license, a vice from the good-old-days he kept for sentimental sake, and a full pound of coke — his personal stash of blow. This was after Russo had bargained with Gravnick, naming Franko Pistale as the man who ordered the hit on his grandfather, Don Caesar Casilone. The same attack in which Ernie's father, Jesse Gravnick was killed. Russo never admitted to ordering the hit on Giaconte, Jr. or the bungled hit on Gravnick, that killed Julie. But Ernie knew it was him. During his questioning of Russo, Gravnick asked if he had ever heard about a so-called hit man called the Ghost. Russo knew all about him — more than he would ever admit.

—◦◦—

Julie left her entire fortune to Ernie, including her beloved home Bella Vista. Winton Cosmetics, International, Inc. would continue to operate under its newly elected CEO, Jennie Mae Wooten. The confiscated shares of Winton Stock were returned to the company.

Having vowed to catch Julie's killer, "no matter what it takes," Gravnick resigned as Chief of Police and Chief of Detectives of the Highland Park Police Department. He would open an office and operate as a licensed Private Investigator in his on-going search for the Ghost, aka the Spook, who no one knew as Roy.

When Sampson heard of Gravnick's resignation, he immediately asked to join him. Gravnick was delighted. He was going to need someone with Sampson's investigative skills. Jack Dilly was named interim Chief of the Highland Park Police Department, and the most likely candidate to get the job permanently. Captain Charley House congratulated Gravnick on his new venture and offered his support.

Gravnick offered Mrs. Den a big raise if she would stay on in her position. He and Jonathan would be needing her to run the house and care for their needs for a long time to come.

—ↄⓖↄ—

At dinner that evening Jonathan told Ernie that he wished to honor his mother by learning more about Judaism. He wanted to study Hebrew and prepare himself to become a Bar Mitzvah. His mom had involved herself in Judaism, to help show him a spiritual path. He would do this for her.

Dora Gravnick and retired senator, Sir Harry Winton returned to the Deerfield Nursing Home where they continue their verbal dual with each other to this day.

ONE YEAR LATER

On a cloudless, Shabbat Saturday morning at the site of the western wall — the holy ancient Temple Mount in Jerusalem, Israel, Rabbi Richard Hirsch directed the bar mitzvah of Jonathan Winton Gravnick. Standing in attendance was his father, Ernie Gravnick, who had been given the great honor of holding the Torah, which had been carefully lifted from its bejeweled, cylindrical case.

Though Bar Mitzvah means 'the coming of age' and is generally performed when a young man reaches age 13, it may take place at a later time. Jonathan was already 15 when he first learned that he was Jewish. He was 16 when his bar mitzvah took place.

Flying home on ELAL at 36,000 plus feet above the Atlantic Ocean, Jonathan exclaimed, "Dad, I've decided, that after I graduate from college, I'm going to become a cop like you. Together we'll make a hell of a team.

ACKNOWLEDGMENTS

In writing this story, I found it takes more than just an author to bring a book to fruition. If it had not been for other people's patience, prodding and faith in me, Gravnick, would never have taken life.

To begin with I want to thank all the members my Thursday morning writer's critique group, who have listened and questioned and taught me so much. Especially, my longtime friend Ron Kenney, who first introduced me to the group. The amazing DJ Towle, who inspires me just by being who she is. Who, can dissect and tear a work apart, suggest changes, and miraculously, leave the writer feeling uplifted. Teresa Bruce, whose edits and comments have made me a better writer. Bob Coombs, who above all others, keeps me honest.

I must also thank Gerry and Lorry Hausman and Alice Carney, for their inspiring leadership of the Green River Writers Workshop. When I was at my lowest ebb, they pumped me up and gave me hope. I give extra thanks to Gerry and Lorry. As my publishers at Irie Books, your patience with me as a first time author, has been astounding.

Not least of all is Sandra Manning, who has been there for me through so many ventures over the years. Thanks for always bailing me out. You are like family.

To my most wonderful and cherished friend, Sandy Silbert, thank you dear Sandy for caring and believing in me. You make me feel like there is nothing I can't do.

Last, but not least, thank you to the readers, who hung in there to the end. The words came from a place deep within me. I hope they touched a place within you.